KNOCKOUT

Fargo didn't bother going for his Colt. It was under his rain-soaked slicker, and by the time he got it out, Bollen and Powell would have filled him full of holes. He needed something to distract them, and he didn't know what it might be.

Jezebel did. She threw the lantern at the twisted trunk of the oak tree. Glass smashed against wood. There was a fiery flash of coal oil, and then darkness.

Fargo threw the slicker aside and grabbed the Colt. He was about to pull the trigger on Bollen when something smashed into the side of his head.

He fell to his knees and was hit again. Fighting the blackness, he collapsed into the hole where the treasure had been, landing with a muddy splash at the bottom, and that was the last thing he knew for quite a while. . . .

D1565346

THE
TRAILSMAN
#246

TEXAS
DEATH STORM

by

Jon Sharpe

A SIGNET BOOK

JH JM

SIGNET
Published by New American Library, a division of
Penguin Putnam Inc., 375 Hudson Street,
New York, New York 10014, U.S.A.
Penguin Books Ltd, 80 Strand,
London WC2R 0RL, England
Penguin Books Australia Ltd, Ringwood,
Victoria, Australia
Penguin Books Canada Ltd, 10 Alcorn Avenue,
Toronto, Ontario, Canada M4V 3B2
Penguin Books (N.Z.) Ltd, 182–190 Wairau Road,
Auckland 10, New Zealand

Penguin Books Ltd, Registered Offices:
Harmondsworth, Middlesex, England

First published by Signet, an imprint of New American Library,
a division of Penguin Putnam Inc.

First Printing, April 2002
10 9 8 7 6 5 4 3 2 1

Copyright © Jon Sharpe, 2002

All rights reserved
The first chapter of this title originally appeared in *Bloody Brazos*,
the two hundred forty-fifth volume in this series.

ⓊREGISTERED TRADEMARK—MARCA REGISTRADA

Printed in the United States of America

Without limiting the rights under copyright reserved above, no part of this
publication may be reproduced, stored in or introduced into a retrieval
system, or transmitted, in any form, or by any means (electronic, mechanical,
photocopying, recording, or otherwise), without the prior written permission
of both the copyright owner and the above publisher of this book.

PUBLISHER'S NOTE
This is a work of fiction. Names, characters, places, and incidents either are
the product of the author's imagination or are used fictitiously, and any re-
semblance to actual persons, living or dead, events, or locales is entirely coin-
cidental.

BOOKS ARE AVAILABLE AT QUANTITY DISCOUNTS WHEN USED TO PROMOTE PRODUCTS
OR SERVICES. FOR INFORMATION PLEASE WRITE TO PREMIUM MARKETING DIVISION,
PENGUIN PUTNAM INC., 375 HUDSON STREET, NEW YORK, NEW YORK 10014.

If you purchased this book without a cover you should be aware that this
book is stolen property. It was reported as "unsold and destroyed" to the
publisher and neither the author nor the publisher has received any payment
for this "stripped book."

The Trailsman

Beginnings . . . they bend the tree and they mark the man. Skye Fargo was born when he was eighteen. Terror was his midwife, vengeance his first cry. Killing spawned Skye Fargo, ruthless, cold-blooded murder. Out of the acrid smoke of gunpowder still hanging in the air, he rose, cried out a promise never forgotten.

The Trailsman they began to call him all across the West: searcher, scout, hunter, the man who could see where others only looked, his skills for hire but not his soul, the man who lived each day to the fullest, yet trailed each tomorrow. Skye Fargo, the Trailsman, the seeker who could take the wildness of a land and the wanting of a woman and make them his own.

Texas, 1860—
Buried gold leads men to an island paradise,
where greed and deception turn nirvana into
a raging hell of blood and murder.

1

Skye Fargo sat astride his big Ovaro stallion and looked up at the tall green pine trees along the trail outside of Huntsville, Texas. Not so long ago, the trail had been used mainly by the Indians, but now settlers were coming in with their wagons. The trail was getting worn and rutted. Fargo wasn't sure he approved of the change.

Somewhere back to the north of him was the state's prison. Fargo had heard tales of the way things were there: the tiny, dark cells that held three or four men; the brutal guards who enjoyed beating the convicts; the food that seemed almost alive because of the maggots that crawled in it.

A hell of a place, Fargo thought, *a lot different from a peaceful trail among the towering pines with the cloudless blue sky overhead.* A man could feel mighty free and easy on the trail, with money in his pocket from the last job he'd done and a little time on his hands. Fargo had both money and time, and he planned to ride down to the Gulf of Mexico and smell the tangy breeze again, maybe even take a swim in the salty water and taste it on his tongue.

A scream cut through the quiet air and shredded Fargo's pleasant thoughts. A hawk burst upward from one of the tallest pines and the treetop shook.

Fargo's lake-blue eyes narrowed and turned cold as ice. At first he thought the scream might have come from a panther, but the pinto didn't turn a hair. Fargo knew that, if a panther was around, the big horse would show some signs of nervousness.

When the scream came again, Fargo knew it was the scream of a woman. Abruptly, it was cut off, as if someone

1

had clamped a hand over the woman's mouth. Silence settled over everything, and the hawk now circled above.

Fargo didn't like to go mixing in the problems of others without knowing what the situation was, and he didn't like walking blindly into a situation that he knew nothing about. But the scream might have signaled distress, meaning that someone could be in big trouble. It wasn't his trouble—not yet—but it paid a man to be careful.

Shifting on the hand-tooled saddle of Mexican leather, Fargo eased the pinto down the trail, looking at the tracks in the dirt. His keen eyes noted that at least three other horses had been there ahead of him that morning, and not long before. Fargo rode slowly, hoping to see where the other horses had left the trail and headed for the trees.

Before he reached that spot, however, he saw movement at the edge of the pines. The lower boughs shook, and a running figure burst out of the trees. Fargo was about a hundred yards away, but even at that distance he could tell that the figure was a woman by the way she ran. She was wearing men's clothing, including a red-and-white shirt, and her long dark hair was tied back in a thick braid that bounced up from her neck with every step she took. She was tall and lithe, and she ran easily, taking long strides through the tall grass that rippled in the slight breeze.

Pursuing her was a short, heavyset man whose thick legs pumped with the effort of each step as he tried to keep up. He laughed as he ran and called to the woman, who ignored him. He ran clumsily, as if under a strain, and he was losing ground with every step until the woman stumbled. She lunged forward and almost fell. She caught herself almost instantly, and after staggering for several yards, she recovered her form. But by then the man was almost within reach of her. He threw himself at her and managed to get a hand on her shirt. As he fell, he pulled her down into the long grass with him.

Fargo watched all of this dispassionately. If a man and a woman wanted to play a little game of slap-and-tickle in the woods, that was all right with him. They'd probably taken a picnic lunch into the woods and then gotten a little frisky. He thought now that the scream may have been one of pleasure rather than distress, cut off with a kiss instead of a hand. He'd heard plenty of women cry out in pleasure, and you could never be sure what kind of sound they'd make. The two people rolling around in the grass would most likely be a little embarrassed to be caught at their game by a stranger, but that wasn't Fargo's problem. He touched his spurs gently to the pinto's flanks and started forward.

Just as he did, the woman screamed again. This time there was no doubt about it. She wasn't taking any pleasure in what was happening. No matter how things had begun, they'd turned ugly.

Fargo thought he'd better take a hand. It was one thing to get caught up in an innocent sex game, but it was something else again to take a woman against her will. He rode to where the grass was thrashing near the trail, and was about to dismount when a movement on the edge of the trees caught his eye. He turned in the saddle for a better look and saw someone else come out of the woods.

It was another man, and this one was riding a big black mare. The man held the reins in his left hand and a pistol in his right. Fargo saw smoke puff from the pistol barrel and heard the blast. There was another shot, and he felt something hit his shoulder like the kick of a government mule, knocking him off the pinto and to the ground.

He landed on his back, his fall hardly cushioned by the grass, and the air was forced from his lungs by the impact. Gasping for breath, his head swimming, he nevertheless struggled to his feet, pulling the Colt from its holster at his side.

All the time he was thinking, *this is what comes of mixing in other people's trouble.*

He had the pistol up and cocked when the man who'd been chasing the woman hit him from behind, slamming into his back with a hard, broad shoulder, throwing him forward and down, and knocking the air out of him again.

Fargo hit the ground and rolled. Somehow he managed to hold on to the Colt, and this time he didn't even try to get up. When he came to a stop, he flopped over on his belly and snapped off a shot at the rider.

He missed, naturally enough. It was hard enough to hit a moving target if you were perfectly steady yourself, and it was damn near impossible after you'd been shot, fallen off a horse, been knocked down again, and rolled five yards.

Fargo stayed down, looking for the squat man, but he was nowhere to be seen. There was a scream from the woman, and Fargo figured the man had gone back to what he was doing, thinking that Fargo must be done for.

The was where he was wrong. Fargo stood up. His knees were a little weak, but they held him.

The rider was almost on him now. He had his gun aimed straight at Fargo, and he was too close to miss. But then so was Fargo, who pulled the trigger of the Colt twice.

The gun jumped in Fargo's hand and both bullets smacked into the rider's chest, throwing him out of the saddle. His horse kept on coming, however, and Fargo had to jump aside to avoid being run down. As he was picking himself up yet again, the squat man landed on his back.

Fargo tried to turn over, but the man held him flat. He smelled of body odor and bad whiskey, and he had a grip like iron. He got a forearm under Fargo's chin and tightened his hold, cutting off Fargo's air supply. With his other hand, he reached out and grabbed Fargo's wrist. When he had a firm grip, he smashed Fargo's hand into the ground, trying to make him drop the Colt.

Fargo hung on. His lungs felt as if they were on fire, and he tried to suck air into them. Though it felt as if his throat was caught in a vise, he didn't let go of the pistol.

The man lowered his head and bit Fargo on the shoulder where he'd been shot.

A red haze filmed Fargo's vision. His fingers went limp, and the gun finally dropped to the ground. He couldn't breathe, and he didn't think he'd last much longer.

But then the iron grip on his neck loosened. The weight rolled off his back. Fargo sucked air and dust into his raw throat. He coughed, breathed again, and coughed some more.

When he could sit up, he saw that the squat man was standing a couple of feet away. The woman he'd been chasing was also standing nearby. She had Fargo's Colt and she was pointing it at the man who'd been chasing her.

"Don't move, Mr. Powell," she told him. "If you do, I'll kill you."

"I don't think so," Powell said. His voice was surprisingly high for a man built like a barrel with legs. "I don't think you'd want to hurt a man just for tryin' to have a little fun."

"Maybe you thought it would be fun," the woman said. "I didn't. Maybe I should just kill you anyway."

That sounded like a damned good idea to Fargo. Powell was quick, and he was tricky. Best to kill him where he stood, before he got the upper hand again.

Fargo opened his mouth to say so, but no words came out. Instead, he made a sound a little like the cawing of an old, tired crow.

The sound was just enough to distract the woman, whose eyes drifted off Powell's face for less than a second. It was all the time that Powell needed. Quick as a cat, he sprang for her, slapping the pistol from her hand and putting a shoulder into her chest. He was about to make a grab for the pistol when he turned to check on Fargo, who had crawled over to the big Ovaro and pulled himself upright. He was about to slide the big Henry rifle from its scabbard, so Powell left the pistol where it was lying, ran to the black mare, and pulled himself into the saddle. He slapped the reins and dug in his heels. The big black horse jumped forward and broke into a run.

Fargo got the Henry out, but he didn't bother to shoot. He was still winded and shaken, not to mention shot and bitten. Shooting at Powell would just be wasting a bullet.

He slid the rifle back into the scabbard and leaned against the pinto. The woman was standing over the man Fargo had shot, pointing the pistol down at his head.

"Don't waste the bullet," Fargo croaked. "He won't get any deader."

The woman held the pistol steady for a while. Then she nodded and moved it, holding it down by her leg.

"Are you all right?" she asked.

Fargo managed a grin. His throat was feeling better, but his voice still came out sounding like a frog with pneumonia.

"Do I look all right?" he asked.

The woman gave him an appraising look with her big black eyes and he looked right back. She was a fine figure of a woman, nearly as tall as Fargo himself, with proud high breasts that her loose man's shirt couldn't hide. Her cotton denim pants fit her in a way that emphasized the curve of her hips and her fine, tight rump. Her lips were a little too full, and her sensuous mouth a little too wide, but she was a beauty, all right. No mistaking that.

"You'll do," she said.

"So will you," Fargo croaked.

"What's that supposed to mean?"

"Whatever you want it to," Fargo said. His voice was already getting stronger. "Who were those two men, and what the hell was going on here?"

"It's a long story."

"I have time."

"You certainly do. You're not going anywhere for a while, not with that shoulder wound."

"I'm not worried so much about the wound," Fargo said. "What I'm worried about is the bite."

"Bite?"

"That fella you called Powell bit me. Right where I was shot."

"That man's mouth is dirtier than a dog's," the woman said. "We have to get that wound cleaned out. Can you get on that horse?"

"I think so," Fargo said.

"Then do it, and follow me."

She handed Fargo his pistol and started walking toward the trees without looking back. Fargo stood beside the pinto for a moment, watching her. Then he pulled himself up into the saddle.

"What's your name?" he called after her.

The woman didn't stop walking. She didn't even look back.

"Jezebel," she said. "Jezebel Carson."

"Nice name," Fargo said.

This time, Jezebel Carson didn't answer. She just kept on making long strides toward the pines.

For a couple of seconds, Fargo admired the way her backside worked inside the tight pants. Then he clucked to the pinto and followed her.

2

"You didn't tell me *your* name," Jezebel said as she cleaned the wound in Fargo's shoulder with whiskey from a bottle that had been lying in a small clearing in the woods.

The clearing had been formed when lightning struck a tall pine, splitting it. It had fallen and taken a couple of smaller trees down with it. There were two horses tied to a dead limb of the large tree, and one of them flicked its tail at a fly buzzing around in the still air.

It was cool in the shade of the clearing, cooler than it had been out on the trail at any rate. The sunlight slanted in through the pines here and there, falling in bright patches on the ground.

"My name's Skye," Fargo said. "Skye Fargo."

"A pleasure, Skye," Jezebel said. "Now tell me if this hurts too much."

The whiskey stung, but Fargo didn't really notice, not so much because he was impervious to pain as because of the way the soft mounds of Jezebel's breasts felt as they pushed against his back.

"That feels just fine," he said. "Be sure you get it clean."

"You don't have to worry about that. You're lucky that bullet just plowed along the top of your shoulder. Lute meant to kill you."

"He'd have to be pretty good to kill me," Fargo said, "shooting from the back of a running horse the way he was. There aren't many men that good."

"Are you?" Jezebel asked.

"Am I what?"

"That good."

7

"Sometimes," Fargo said. "Who the hell was that fella, any-way?"

"Lute Hawkins," Jezebel said. "The other one was Sim Powell. Now hold still. I have to bandage that wound."

She went to get some clean cloth from the saddlebags of one of the horses. Fargo watched her move. He wondered if the sensual motion of her hips was a show for him, or if it was just natural. Either way, it was something fine to see.

When she had his shoulder bandaged, Fargo put his shirt back on. He noticed her watching him with almost as much appreciation as he had watched her.

"Now that I think of it," she said, "your name sounds famil-iar for some reason. Should I have heard of you?"

"Probably not."

"Fargo," she said. "Fargo. Now I remember. Are you the one they call the Trailsman?"

"Some folks call me that."

"I wish I'd met you sooner. Then I could have hired you in-stead of Hawkins and Powell."

"You never did tell me who Hawkins was," Fargo said.

"Yes, I did."

"You told me his name. It's not the same thing."

"Oh. I see what you mean. Well, it's dangerous to travel alone—especially for a woman, and especially around here. Sometimes men escape from the prison, and when they do they prey on people passing through. I was a little worried about that, so I hired Hawkins and Powell to see me safe to Galveston. Like I said, I wish I'd hired you instead."

Fargo wondered if she might be hinting. Well, he was going to Galveston anyway, and he had a feeling she would make a mighty interesting traveling companion.

"Seems like Hawkins and Powell decided to prey on you," he said. "But they weren't escaped prisoners, were they?"

"As far as I know, they weren't," Jezebel said. "But they were lying bastards. They told me they thought someone was following us, probably someone who'd escaped from the prison. And I believed them, fool that I was. All they wanted to do was get me off the trail and into the woods so they could have a little fun. Oh, my God!"

She turned and ran to one of the horses and began digging around in the saddlebags.

"The dirty, filthy bastards!" she screamed. "They stole it! Quick! We have to get Hawkins's body!"

"What for? What's all the yelling about?"

"Never mind. Just come on."

Jezebel untied the reins of the horse whose saddlebags she'd been searching, put her foot in the stirrup, and swung herself up. Fargo admired the ease with which she did it. She didn't say anything else. She just rode away without turning her head.

Fargo shrugged and, using his good arm, pulled himself up onto the pinto. He was curious to see what all the hurry was about. Hawkins wasn't going anywhere, after all.

When he reached the body, Jezebel was already off her horse, shooing away a big black buzzard that had begun to feed on Hawkins's remains. The buzzard hopped to one side, but he didn't fly off. Buzzards were patient birds and this one seemed willing to wait its turn.

A cloud of flies lifted off Hawkins's shattered chest as Jezebel knelt beside him. The flies buzzed around her head, and she brushed angrily at them with one hand as she ran her other hand over Hawkins's bloody shirt.

"It has to be here," she said. "It has to."

"What the hell are you looking for?" Fargo asked, watching her. His voice was better, his throat not feeling quite as raw, but his shoulder was beginning to throb a bit.

"I'm looking for my map," Jezebel said. "It was in my saddlebags, and now it's gone. Now I know what took Hawkins so long to come after me. He was looking for the map. He must've found it. He wouldn't have left without it."

"You don't need a map to get to Galveston," Fargo said. "This trail here goes right on down to Houston. After that, you can catch the train."

"You don't understand," Jezebel said. A sob caught at her voice, and she started pulling at the dead man's pockets. "You don't understand."

She was right. Fargo didn't understand. But then he was a man who didn't have much use for maps. He followed trails when they were there, and when they weren't, well, he made his own. He didn't need any maps to guide him. He watched Jezebel paw frantically at Hawkins's clothing and wondered if she was crazy. He wondered if it might not be a good idea for him just to ride on down the trail alone.

The buzzard sat watching, its eyes steady, its head cocked a little to the side. It didn't move.

After a few more seconds of searching, Jezebel pulled something out of one of Hawkins's pockets and looked at it.

"Thank God," she said. "I found it."

It didn't look like much of a map from what Fargo could see of it, just a tattered old piece of paper, folded into a square. The edges were frayed as if from a lot of handling.

"We have to get out of here," Jezebel said. "Right now."

She jammed the paper in her own pocket and got on her horse.

"Are you coming or not?" she asked Fargo.

"I'm not sure," he said. "You're in a powerful hurry all of a sudden. You seem to be forgetting that there's a dead man here. And there's a horse back there in the woods."

"Of course. We can't leave the horse. But I don't see why we can't leave Hawkins. He tried to kill you, and he was going to let Powell rape me. He'd have taken his turn afterward, too. You can bet on that."

Fargo looked down into Hawkins's wide-open eyes. There was nothing there to tell what kind of man Hawkins had been, but Fargo didn't see any reason to doubt what Jezebel said. Still, it wasn't a good idea to leave a dead man lying out like that. People might get the wrong idea about what had happened, and Fargo didn't want to have to deal with the law, no matter how slight the chances of it seemed.

"We can't just leave him lying here," Fargo said.

Jezebel shook her head. "Yes, we can. The buzzards will take care of him."

The one buzzard that was already there had taken a couple of steps closer to the body as they talked.

"We have to hurry," Jezebel told Fargo. "Powell will be back. He might be on the way here now."

"Why?"

"The map. He'll be back for the map as soon as he thinks about it."

"Doesn't matter," Fargo said. "We're not going off and leaving this body here. We'll drag him back to the trees."

Jezebel looked for a second as if she might protest, but then she said, "All right. But we have to hurry."

"It won't take long," Fargo said. "And after we get him there, we'll have a little talk about that map of yours."

He tossed Jezebel the end of his lasso, and she tied it around Hawkins's feet. When it was secure, Fargo started off. Hawkins bumped along behind, little puffs of dust rising as his head hit the rough spots. Fargo didn't feel bad about dragging him, though. After all, Hawkins had tried to kill him. No need to feel sorry for someone like that.

The buzzard watched them go.

Back in the clearing, Fargo and Jezebel untied Hawkins and tied the third horse behind Fargo's Ovaro. Then they rode away, leaving Hawkins lying on the forest floor. They didn't even throw any pine needles over him.

Fargo knew they should have buried him. He wasn't being sentimental about it. It was just a practical matter. Several buzzards were already circling over the trees, probably including the one they'd shooed away from the body to begin with. Maybe people passing along the trail would think there was just some dead animal back in the pines. That would be fine. But maybe someone would be curious enough to investigate. Fargo would just as soon that didn't happen.

"Let's get out of here," Jezebel said. "We need to find a place to stay by tonight, some place where Powell can't get at us."

"If a man wants to get at you, he can," Fargo said. "No matter where you're staying."

"But you won't let him, will you? You'll take care of me?"

Fargo hesitated before answering, and Jezebel said, "If it's money you want, I can pay you."

"It's not the money," Fargo said.

"What then?"

"That map, for one thing. I want to know about the map."

"I should never have mentioned it. If I hadn't told Powell about it, he might have left me alone."

"You can trust me."

"I thought I could trust Powell," Jezebel said, "but I was wrong."

"That must be one hell of a map," Fargo said.

Jezebel nodded. "It is. It really is."

"Since I already know how much it means to you, you might as well go on and tell me."

"First you have to agree to guide me to Galveston."

"I can do that, but I've already told you: You don't need a guide."

"You also have to protect me from Powell. And from anyone else."

Fargo wondered who "anyone else" might be, but he didn't ask, though he knew he'd have to find out eventually. "I'll do my best," he said. "Now tell me about the map."

"I can talk while we ride," Jezebel said, heading her horse out of the clearing.

Fargo followed her, and when they were on the trail, he rode up beside her.

"Time to start talking," he said.

"All right. What do you know about Jean Lafitte?"

"The pirate?"

"Privateer," Jezebel said. "He wasn't a pirate."

"Don't see that there was much difference," Fargo told her. "Anyway, I don't know much about him at all except that he lived on Galveston Island for a while."

"That's all you need to know. That, and the fact that he buried his treasure there. The map I have isn't for finding the island. Anybody can do that. But not just anybody can find the treasure. For that, you need a map."

"And you have one."

"Yes. And Powell knows it. That's why he'll be back."

Fargo had been hearing of treasure for most of his life: lost mines, gold left behind by the conquistadors, plunder hidden by pirates. The thing was, while he'd heard about all that treasure lying hidden in the earth or in caves or in lost cities, he'd never heard of anyone who'd found any of it.

"You can see why I need your help, can't you?" Jezebel asked.

Fargo said he could see, all right.

"And you'll help me get to Galveston?"

Fargo didn't see any reason why not. He didn't think she'd ever find any treasure, but that wasn't his problem.

"I'll help you," he said.

"After we get there, I might need some more help."

"What kind of help?"

Jezebel hesitated just long enough to make Fargo wonder if she was going to tell him the truth.

"Nothing difficult," she said. "Just locating landmarks, things like that. A man called the Trailsman should be able to do that without any trouble."

"Landmarks on an island don't always stay the same," Fargo said. "Storms come along and change things."

"Of course. That's why I might need your help."

"We can talk about that when we get there," Fargo said, wondering why it was that he didn't believe she was being entirely truthful with him.

"I can assure you that I'd be grateful," she said. "Very grateful."

Fargo gave her a look, and she held his gaze.

"Well, now, that sounds like an interesting proposition," he said.

"It will be more than interesting," she said. "I can promise you that."

"We'll see, then," Fargo told her.

3

The place where they stopped for the night was like a lot of other places Fargo had seen. It called itself a saloon, but it wasn't much better than a trading post. However, it had the advantage of being the only place to stop for miles around.

Inside the ramshackle building a crude bar was formed by a couple of planks atop some barrels, three roughly built tables with rickety chairs, and an owner who didn't care what kind of customers he got as long as they could pay for the cheap whiskey he served. The floor was hard-packed dirt, and nothing in the place was any too clean.

There were three men at the bar when Fargo and Jezebel walked in, and when the door swung open the men turned to see who had entered. When they saw Jezebel they elbowed each other and made muffled comments that must have been funny—at least to them. One of them laughed aloud.

The one who laughed was tall—taller than Fargo—and solid. He wore a floppy hat and clothes that were powdered with trail dust. Fargo couldn't see his face. He had a matted beard, and the brim of the hat hid his eyes in shadow. He said something to the others, and they laughed with him.

Fargo paid them no mind. He walked up to the bar and stood a little away from the men, who didn't seem to notice him at all. They were still looking at Jezebel, who stood beside the door and ignored their stares.

The bartender, who was also the owner, was fat and hairy. He wore his shirt with the top two buttons undone, and thick tufts of gray hair stuck out of the V of the neckline. His stomach bulged behind a dirty apron that might have been white at one time but was now mostly gray and covered with unidentifiable stains.

"What's your pleasure?" the bartender asked, eyeing the torn shoulder of Fargo's shirt and the piece of bandage that showed through the hole.

"We'd like to camp here for the night," Fargo said. "That be all right with you?"

"Won't bother me none. Don't have any rooms, if that's what you're looking for."

Fargo said he didn't need a room.

"Then you're welcome. You can pitch a tent if you want to. Couple of nice spots outside."

Fargo didn't think Jezebel had a tent, but he'd noticed a big oak tree nearby. Sleeping beneath it wouldn't be too bad.

"Can we get something to eat?" he asked.

"We got beefsteak and potatoes. My wife can cook it up, if you want it."

He didn't make it sound very appetizing, but Fargo believed in eating real food when you had the chance. Fried biscuits and other kinds of trail food were fine when you couldn't get anything else, but when you had an opportunity to get something a little more substantial, you took it.

"We want it," he said.

He walked to one of the tables, pulled out a chair, and motioned for Jezebel to come over. He held the chair for her, which brought another round of raucous laughter from the men at the bar.

The owner went into a back room and called out something to his wife. When he returned, he came over to Fargo's table and said in a voice that couldn't be heard at the bar, "Don't let those fellas bother you none. Just trail trash passing through. You want a drink to go with that steak?"

"Whiskey," Fargo said, but Jezebel shook her head.

The bartender went back behind the bar, and the men standing there ordered another round.

"I don't like this place," Jezebel said.

Fargo didn't like it much, either, but it was the only place around that offered any kind of protection from the night.

"I thought you were worried about Sim Powell," he said. "I don't think he'll bother us here."

"I'm more worried about those men at the bar than I am about Powell. They look even worse than him."

Fargo didn't like the looks of them, either. They might be trail trash, like the bartender said, but they looked tough, especially the big one with the beard. Fargo wished he could get a look at his eyes. You could tell a lot about a man if you could see his eyes.

The bartender brought Fargo's whiskey and set it on the table. Fargo took a swallow and felt it burn his still-raw throat. It was almost as bad as having Powell's arm around it again.

There was another joke at the bar, and the men turned toward the table. One of them, not the big one, sauntered over to where Fargo and Jezebel were sitting. He was skinny, with a turkey neck and thin arms. His eyes were bloodshot, and he'd clearly been drinking for quite a while.

"You two been on the trail long?" he asked.

Fargo took another drink of whiskey and set the empty glass on the table. He nodded, which might have meant yes or no or anything the man wanted it to mean.

"Must be nice, traveling with a pretty woman," the man said. "Keeps you warm at night, I guess."

Fargo didn't say anything, and the man laid a hand on his shoulder. Fargo shook it off and stood up.

"Nobody puts a hand on me," he said.

Turkey-neck backed away, both hands up, palms outward, walking so that Fargo couldn't see the third man at the bar.

"I didn't mean a thing by it," Turkey-neck said. "Not a thing."

Fargo hooked a foot around one leg of the chair and sent it skidding toward the man. It didn't hit him, but he danced aside far enough for Fargo to see the third man going for his pistol.

Ducking to one side, Fargo pulled his Colt and fired. The man at the bar yelled and dropped his pistol when the bullet hit his arm.

Turkey-neck grabbed the chair and threw it at Fargo, who dodged to his right. He wasn't quite quick enough, though, and the chair leg hit him a glancing blow on the side of the head, throwing him off balance. He fell to the floor and rolled under a table, which was just as well, since Turkey-neck had his own pistol out and was firing at the spot where Fargo had been. A bullet sent dirt flying up from the floor.

Fargo flipped the table over and a second bullet ripped through the top and buzzed by his ear.

Before Fargo could fire a shot, he heard a solid thud, followed by the sound of a body hitting the floor. Looking over the tabletop, Fargo saw Turkey-neck lying stretched out on the dirt. The bartender was standing over him with a bung hammer in one hand and a look of satisfaction on his face.

"I don't like people messing up the place," he said. "I try to keep it nice."

Fargo stood up. He wondered whether the bartender was joking or whether he really meant it. It was hard to tell from his expressionless tone.

"You say you don't like people messing up your place?" the man with the beard said.

The bartender turned to look at him. "That's right."

"Well, I don't like people messing with my men. Looks to me like one of 'em's shot and the other one's gonna have a hell of a headache."

"They shouldn't bother my customers," the bartender said.

Fargo didn't say anything. He just stood there with his pistol held loosely at his side, ready to use it if he had to.

The bearded man walked over to Turkey-neck and prodded him none to gently with the toe of his boot.

"Get your ass up, Willie," he said.

Willie stirred and groaned but didn't get up. The bearded man nudged him again.

"Dammit, Willie, get up!"

Willie got to his knees, then to his feet. He swayed for a second, then walked to a chair and sat down. His eyes were glazed, and Fargo didn't think he knew exactly what was going on or what had happened to him.

The other man was sitting on the floor with his back to one the barrels that held the makeshift bar. There was blood on his shirt. The bearded man turned to him.

"Goddamn, Gar," the man said. "I been shot."

"It's just your arm," Gar said. "Can you move it?"

"I think so."

"Well, move it, goddamn it."

The man moved his arm. He bit his lip to stop a cry of pain from escaping.

17

"Is it broke?" Gar asked.

"Don't think so," the man said.

"Then get up. We're leaving this stinkhole."

"That ain't no way to talk about a man's place," the bartender said, but there was something uneasy in his voice, and his body was tense. "I keep a nice place here."

Gar looked at him. Fargo still couldn't see the man's eyes.

"Like hell you do," Gar said. "Come on, Joe. Willie."

He left the room, trailed by his two men. Willie couldn't quite walk a straight line, and the third man was holding his arm and gritting his teeth. After they'd gone through the door, Gar stuck his head back inside.

"I don't let anybody mess with my men," he said. "Not and get away with it."

Then he was gone.

The bartender's shoulders slumped, and he sighed.

"Shit," he said. "I think I might've made a big mistake by helping you out, stranger."

"Why's that?" Fargo asked.

He looked at his shoulder. It wasn't hurting much more than before, but it had begun bleeding again. Probably wasn't anything to worry about. The wound was shallow, and the bleeding would stop soon. He could change the bandage later, or Jezebel could.

"Didn't you hear what they called that one with the beard?" the bartender asked.

"Gar," Jezebel said.

Fargo turned to her. "So?"

"Gar Bollen," she said. "Ever hear of him?"

"Nope," Fargo said. "Can't say that I have."

"I have," the bartender said. "I need a drink."

He went to the bar, set the bung hammer on it, and grabbed a bottle of whiskey by the neck. As he drank from the bottle, his wife came from the other room with a large white dish in each hand.

"I heard the shooting," she said. "Anybody killed?"

She was a large round woman with a look that said she'd seen it all before and wasn't disturbed by any of it.

"Nobody's killed," Fargo said.

The woman looked around as if to make sure he wasn't

lying. When she saw that the floor was clear of bodies, she said, "Good. These steaks for you two, then?"

"That's right," Fargo told her. "Bring them on over."

She set the plates on the table, and Fargo saw a large, thin steak beside a pile of mashed potatoes and gravy.

"Looks good," he said.

"Better'n nothing," the woman said. "I'll go get you a knife."

She went away and returned with forks, knives, and napkins. As Fargo was tucking his napkin in, she said, "My name's Sue Potter. That's my husband, Dan, over there having himself a drink on the house. What happened in here?"

Fargo didn't think it was his place to explain. He tried cutting the steak. It wasn't as tough as it looked. He sliced off a couple of bites and started eating.

"We had a little trouble with your other customers," Jezebel said. "They weren't very polite."

"Polite, hell," Dan Potter said from the bar. "That there was Gar Bollen and his gang."

His wife wasn't fazed. "Imagine that. Gar Bollen stopping here in our little saloon."

Potter wiped his face with a bar rag. "I never should have hit that man. There's no telling what they'll do."

Fargo stopped eating long enough to say, "They won't do anything. It's not the first time one of 'em got shot or hit in the head."

"You don't know much about Gar Bollen, do you?" Jezebel said.

"Not a thing," Fargo admitted.

"He's got a reputation for being a killer," she said. "There are all sorts of stories about the things he's done in this part of Texas."

"Killed a man once for making fun of that hat of his," Potter said. "Shot him in a saloon down in Houston. Don't that worry you?"

"I didn't make fun of his hat," Fargo said.

He went on with his eating. The potatoes were a little watery and didn't have much taste, but then potatoes never had much taste.

"Well, it worries the hell out of me," Potter said. "I'm glad you two are gonna be camped out here tonight. That way maybe if Bollen comes sneaking back, he'll get his revenge on you and leave me and my place alone."

"I swear, Dan Potter," his wife said, "I never took you for a coward."

"I'm not a coward." Potter drank from the bottle and set it down hard on the bar. "I just don't want to have to stand up to Gar Bollen."

"Seems to me you just did," Fargo reminded him.

Potter thought that over and then said, "Yeah, I guess I did. But I didn't know it at the time."

"You'd have done the same thing even if you'd known," Fargo said.

"I wouldn't count on that," Potter said.

It was near the end of summer and the nights in Southeast Texas were warm and muggy, not the best weather for sleeping outside, or even inside.

"Mosquitos aren't too bad," Sue Potter told Jezebel. "Been too dry for 'em. And if you need to wash up, there's a creek runs through the trees just down that little hill behind the saloon."

Fargo pulled his bedroll off his horse and tossed it on the ground under the oak tree. A bath sounded like a good idea after the time he'd spent rolling around on the ground and Potter's dirty floor.

Jezebel thanked Mrs. Potter, who nodded and went back to join her husband—who by that time would be just about finished with the bottle of whiskey. Fargo thought he'd be passed out soon, if he wasn't already.

"What do you think?" Jezebel asked.

"About what?" Fargo replied.

"About that creek."

"I'm ready when you are."

Jezebel arched an eyebrow. "Pretty sure of yourself, aren't you?"

"Sure? No, I'm not sure. But it seems to me you still haven't thanked me for saving you from Hawkins and Powell. Maybe you've been thinking about how you'd like to do that."

"I bandaged your shoulder."

"And I appreciate it, and I'd appreciate it if you'd change it again after we clean it up. Seems to me that's a mighty weak thanks, though."

Jezebel smiled. "And you think I could come up with something better?"

"I could help you if you wanted me to."

"Oh, I have a feeling I know what you have in mind."

The color was rising in her face, but Fargo didn't think it was due to anger. He decided to find out.

"You thinking that I'm no better than Powell?" he asked.

"No." Jezebel licked her lips and smiled. "Actually, I'll bet you're a lot better than Powell, not that I'd know much about how good he is."

"You don't know about me, either."

"No, but I think I might be about to find out."

"Why don't we go on down to the creek and see if you're right, then."

She turned and walked away from him. Once again, he admired the intriguing motion of her backside. After she'd gone about ten yards, he followed.

4

The water in the creek was warm and muddy. It would have been clearer, Fargo thought, if there'd been more rain, but Texas had been dry that summer. He was sitting out in the middle of the creek, which had shrunk down to about a third of its usual size. Though he was in the deepest part, the water came only up to his shoulders.

It was getting on toward evening, and trees along the creek bank threw a thick shade on the water. Fargo could see the sun through the lower branches as it sank toward the horizon. He sat in the water and waited patiently for Jezebel.

She had insisted that he go in first, while she undressed in private. It didn't matter to Fargo, and he'd been glad to splash a little water on himself and to check his wound. The water was refreshing even if it was muddy, and the wound looked all right. It wasn't bleeding, and it didn't even hurt much, just sort of burned as if he were standing too close to a fire.

Fargo heard a noise on the bank and looked over to where Jezebel was entering the water. She was completely naked, and not a bit ashamed of it. She looked even better than Fargo had thought she would. Her breasts were large and firm, tipped with large, dark nipples that stood out from the two creamy mounds of flesh. Her waist was slim, and her stomach was firm. She had unbraided her black hair, which now hung loosely around her shoulders, and she moved easily on long, slender legs that descended from her tantalizing hips. The bush of black hair that grew between her legs was thick and curly.

She walked into the water and stood with her hands on her hips while she looked boldly at Fargo.

"This water's not deep enough to hide much," she said.

22

Fargo, who felt his manhood growing rigid, said, "It's hiding one thing I can think of."

"Maybe you're ashamed of it."

Fargo stood up, water running down over his body and splashing back into the creek.

Jezebel looked at him appraisingly. "On the other hand, you don't have a thing to be ashamed of."

She turned to the side and hit the water in a shallow dive, kicking her feet and sliding along just beneath the surface like a large, pale fish. She scooted past Fargo and headed down the middle of the creek.

The Trailsman reached out and caught her ankle, bringing her to a stop. She turned and surfaced when he released her, tossing her wet black hair and scattering water drops that dimpled the surface around her.

"I really do appreciate you saving me from Hawkins and Powell," she said, slicking back her hair with both hands. "It's not that I don't like men. I do, but only the ones I choose. I'd never choose a pig like Powell."

"So you've thought of a way to show your appreciation?"

"I cleaned your wound, and now you've seen me naked. Do you want more?"

Fargo reached down and took her hand, pulling her up so that she was standing in front of him.

"You know what I want," he said.

She pressed herself against him. He felt the hot hard tips of her breasts burn against his chest.

"Take it then," she said.

Fargo kissed her, and her mouth opened under his, her tongue darting between his teeth to tease him. While they were still embracing, she reached down with one hand to feel the firmness of his manhood, giving it a light squeeze.

Fargo broke the kiss, but Jezebel kept her grip on him, moving her hand up and down his steely shaft.

"Is this what you had in mind?" she asked.

"Not exactly," Fargo said. "Not that it doesn't feel mighty nice."

"Why don't we go up on the grass where you can make me feel nice, too," she said, leading him out of the creek.

When they reached the bank, she took him behind a bush,

23

and Fargo saw that she had spread a blanket on the ground while she was undressing.

"You plan ahead," Fargo said.

"Maybe I'm just sure of myself," Jezebel said, lying down on the blanket. "Why don't you join me?"

It sounded like a good idea to Fargo, but he stood there for a moment, admiring her. She was a large woman, but she was perfectly proportioned, from the ample breasts to the tapered waist to the long, shapely legs.

"You like what you see?" she asked.

"You could say that."

Fargo knelt beside her and began to stroke her body with feathery touches, letting his fingers roam from the erect nipples to her taut stomach. After a few seconds of that, his hand drifted lower and caressed her wiry pubic hair.

She arched her back and pressed her mound against his hand, but he brought it back to her breasts, teasing each nipple to even greater hardness. Then he began to lick them, circling them gently with his tongue and finally taking one into his mouth, sucking it until Jezebel began to pant. Her body was writhing with pleasure, and she took his hand and placed it on her mound. This time he let his finger find the moist opening and slide inside.

"Ahhhhh," Jezebel said.

She propped herself on her elbows, her head thrown back, her mouth open, her eyes closed.

Fargo let his finger move slowly. After only a few seconds, her hips began to rise up and down. Each time, she thrust them harder against Fargo's hand as her breath came faster and faster.

When he saw that she was about to explode, he moved his hand, but she gripped his wrist and held him in place. Even in the twilight, he could see the color that flooded her face and the flush that spread across her breasts. A shudder began at her toes and passed all the way up her body, and when it reached her shoulders, she cried out.

It wasn't a scream of distress like the one Fargo had heard when Powell was trying to force himself on her. It was a cry of sensual joy.

Jezebel's body went still, and she lay back on the blanket, looking at Fargo with hooded eyes.

"There aren't many men who could do that to me," she said. "Not with just a hand."

She turned over on him and took him in her mouth. He felt the warm moistness of her lips and tongue as they lathered the length of his shaft, and his hands tangled in her hair as she moved skillfully up and down, all the while making noises of satisfaction deep in her throat.

Now it was Fargo who was about to explode, but she didn't give him the chance. She moved her head away and said, "I want to feel you inside me."

She lay back, spreading her legs, and Fargo entered her. She was so wet his entire length slid into her in an instant.

"Ohhhhh," she said. "Yesssssss." Her hips began to rotate beneath him so rapidly that he knew she would reach her climax in mere moments.

He felt the tension begin to grow in his calves, but he held himself back until she began to shudder again. Then, before she could go limp, he started to move with long slow strokes that grew faster and faster. She seemed surprised at first, but then joined in with enthusiasm, and the two of them reached the height of their pleasure at the same moment, Fargo firing into her round after round of the stuff of himself as she clawed his back and kissed him again and again.

When they were both lying exhausted on the blanket, Jezebel touched Fargo's face and said, "I hope you consider yourself properly thanked."

"Oh, I do," he said. "Properly, but not sufficiently, if you know what I mean."

"My God, do you mean you can go again?"

"What do you think?"

"You know," she said, "I think you can."

And he did.

Fargo slept the sleep of the just and the satisfied that night, his blanket not far from Jezebel's, but not touching it. She didn't seem to need him too close, and that was fine with Fargo. He liked women. He liked them a lot. But he didn't want them clinging to him, and he had no intention of letting

one of them tie him down, not even one as beautiful and intriguing as Jezebel Carson.

Not even if she found Jean Lafitte's treasure.

They weren't disturbed during the night, not that Fargo had
expected anything. He didn't care about Gar Bollen's reputation. If the man had wanted a fight, he could have had one in
the saloon.

Still, Fargo would have liked to see the man's eyes. There
was something sinister in the way he'd kept them hidden, as if
he knew that there was something revealed in his gaze.

Fargo and Jezebel had bacon and biscuits in the saloon for
breakfast. Sue Potter served them, but there was no sign of her
husband.

"He'll be up and around later on," Sue said. "He'll have a
little hair of the dog, and then he'll be fine. He's a good man,
but he's a little worried that Gar Bollen might come back and
shoot up our place. You know why they call him Gar?"

Fargo chewed his bacon. He didn't really care. Names
didn't necessarily mean anything.

Jezebel, however, seemed interested.

"Why?" she asked.

"Well," Sue said, "you know what a gar fish is like, don't
you?"

"Long and toothy," Jezebel said. "Like an alligator."

"That's right," Sue said. "But there's another thing an alligator is, and that's mean. So is Gar Bollen. Long and toothy
and mean. They say he bit a man's nose off in a fight in San
Antonio, bit it off and stood chewing it up while the man
watched him. They say the man was holding his hands to his
face with the blood running through his fingers and screaming
so you'd of thought he was a catamount, looking at Gar Bollen
with eyes as wide as a cat's at night. And all the time Gar was
chewing and grinning. He didn't swallow the nose, though."

"What did he do?" Jezebel asked.

"Spit it out on the ground. A nose is mostly gristle, you
know, and mighty hard chewing, or so I'd guess. I never
chewed on one, myself. Anyway, that's what he did. He spit it
on the ground. Wasn't much left of it, probably. Then he

26

stomped it in the dirt with his boot heel and walked off. Hope this ain't bothering your breakfast, Mr. Fargo."

"Not a bit," Fargo said. "This bacon's not as gristly as a nose."

"I'm glad to hear it. Dan butchered that hog himself."

"What happened to the man whose nose was bitten off?" Jezebel asked.

"Don't know," Sue said. "I'd think it'd be hard to go through life without a nose, though."

"There's things a man would miss more," Fargo said with a grin, and Jezebel kicked him under the table.

Sue Potter grinned, too. "Ain't it the truth," she said.

5

It took Fargo and Jezebel four days to get to Houston, where the air was hot, sticky, and full of mosquitos. No matter how dry it was in other parts of Texas, the Gulf Coast always seemed to get rain. And the rain brought out the mosquitos.

Fargo couldn't see why anyone would want to live in such a place, but apparently plenty of people did. The streets were bustling and crowded, and Fargo was glad they wouldn't be staying there. He didn't like cities.

Galveston was a city, too, of course, but it wasn't like Houston. It was prosperous, but not everyone seemed in such a hurry. The Queen City of Texas, they called it, and it was probably the most important in the state, thanks to all of the cotton and other goods that passed through it on the way to other ports.

Fargo saw to the stabling of his horse before he and Jezebel took the train to the island. That was another thing he didn't like: leaving his horse behind. But it would be for only a short while, and he made sure the pinto would be well taken care of. Jezebel sold both the horse she was riding and the one that Powell had left behind.

"I'll pay the bill for your horse in advance," she told Fargo, and went off to make the deal with the livery's owner.

Fargo wondered how long she'd tell him that the horse would be staying, but he didn't ask.

At the depot on the edge of town, Fargo and Jezebel boarded one of the passenger cars of the Galveston, Houston, and Henderson Railroad Company. The car wasn't as fancy as some Fargo had seen in his travels, but it would do fine. The trip to Galveston wouldn't take too long, and he was looking forward to crossing the bay and seeing the wide stretch of water.

The train got under way amid much chuffing and hissing and steaming, and soon the soothing sound of the wheels clicking over the tracks was enough to make Fargo want to lean back in his seat and close his eyes. But he didn't. Instead, he listened in on the conversation of the two men in the seat behind him. They were talking loudly, as if impressed by the sound of their own voices. They didn't impress Fargo, but he wanted to hear about Galveston. It seemed that the biggest topic of conversation on the island these days was slavery, and the war that people seemed sure was coming.

"Governor Houston is anti-slavery, of course," one of the men said. "But Texas can't survive without slaves. The cotton trade is the lifeblood of the state, and of Galveston especially. If it comes to a vote, Texas will secede, no matter what Houston says."

"What about the slaves in Galveston?" his companion asked. "What will they do?"

"They'll obey their masters for now," the first man said. "But when the war comes, I don't know what will happen. Galveston is in an exposed position and can't be easily defended from enemies without, much less within."

Jezebel must have been listening, too, because she said quietly to Fargo, "Don't let that war talk bother you. If war does come, it won't come to Texas. Even if it does, it won't come for years. We have plenty of time to get what we came for and leave."

Fargo wasn't worried about war. He'd heard the talk before. He said, "You know, you haven't let me have a look at that map yet. If I'm going to help you, I should know where I'm going to be looking."

Jezebel frowned. "It's not that I don't trust you. But I told Powell too much, and you can see where that got me. I'm sure he and Hawkins would have killed me after they were finished with me. They'd have taken my map and found the treasure themselves."

"You know I don't plan to kill you," Fargo said.

Jezebel grinned wickedly. "Not the way they would have, I'll grant you that."

Fargo had to smile as he thought of their four days of travel. Or the nights. It was the nights that were most worth thinking about, and he'd done his best not to kill Jezebel, but rather to keep her tired out so she could sleep.

"I thought it was the other way around," he said. "I thought you were going to kill me."

"I don't think I could kill a man that way," she said, her face coloring.

"Only one way to find out," Fargo said. "And that's to keep trying."

Jezebel was about to answer, but the bay had come into sight, and they were silent as they looked out at the smooth, flat water. The land they were leaving behind was flat, too, coastal prairie that stretched for miles and miles.

Above them were piles of high, flat-bottomed clouds, and ahead of them was the island. Fargo could see the eastern end of it curving in front of the bay and stretching on down the coastline. It seemed to sit right on top of the water, as if the least little wave that washed ashore from the Gulf would roll right over it.

"It's not as low as it looks," Jezebel said as if reading his thoughts. "But I'd hate to be there during a storm."

"I hear they come along during the summer sometimes," Fargo said, thinking that it was early September now and maybe the storm season was over. Anyway, he wasn't worried about them. If they came, they came.

"Storms mostly come along during the summer, but they come during the fall, too," Jezebel said. "Besides, it's still summer here, or hadn't you noticed?"

Fargo had noticed, all right, but he knew that Galveston wouldn't be as uncomfortable as Houston. The breeze from the Gulf kept the mosquitos down a little, and it helped to cool things off.

"How long will it take us to get set up and start looking for that treasure of yours?" he asked.

"Not long. That is, if nobody tries to stop us."

Fargo's suspicions were aroused. He'd had a feeling all along that there were things Jezebel wasn't telling him, and he knew he'd have to get her to tell him sooner or later. He decided that the time had come.

"I think you've been holding out on me," he said.

Jezebel gave him an innocent look and said, "Why would I do that?"

"That's what I'm wondering. Why don't you start by telling me where you got that map of yours?"

"Why do you want to know?"

"Because it's about time I found out a little more about what I've let myself in for. I admit that it's been nice to travel with you this far, but the truth is, you didn't really need any protection. About the worst thing we've run into is the mosquitos."

"You're forgetting about Gar Bollen."

"No, I'm not. I think Potter could have handled him if I hadn't been there."

"I'm not so sure about that."

"Well," Fargo said, "it doesn't matter now. What matters is that we're getting off the subject. Where did that map come from?"

"Look," Jezebel said. "Seagulls."

She pointed out the window of the rocking train at a flock of gulls that dipped and dived out over the water.

"I've seen birds before," Fargo said. "Quit trying to change the subject. Tell me about that map now, or when I get off this train, you'll never see me again."

"Oh, all right. I got it from my uncle, if you have to know."

"Your uncle?"

"My father's older brother. He was born in Galveston and lived there for a long time, but he bought a cotton plantation up in central Texas years ago. My father sent word that he needed the map, and someone had to go after it. That was me."

"So your father and your uncle were still in touch, but they never saw each other."

"That's right. My uncle might have left Galveston, but that doesn't mean he forgot about us. We used to get letters from him about once a month."

"How did he get the map?"

"Let's just say he knew somebody who trusted him with it."

There were several points of this story that Fargo didn't understand, especially the last one.

"Why didn't he or your father dig for the treasure long ago?"

"Everybody who lives in Galveston has heard stories about Lafitte's treasure, but nobody's ever found it. There are probably a hundred different maps that supposedly show where it is, and not a one of them is genuine. Except maybe the one I have. But it's not really very clear—even from the map—exactly where the treasure is."

"Why is the map so important all of a sudden?" Fargo asked.

"We need the money," Jezebel said. "My father and I."

"Why did he send you? Why not go himself?"

"He had to stay at home."

Getting information from Jezebel had suddenly become as hard as extracting gold from pyrite. Fargo said, "Why did he have to stay?"

"Because of the cattle."

"I think you have a long story to tell me," Fargo said. "And we're nearly at the station."

"We could have something to eat. I'll tell you then."

"You'd better," Fargo said.

6

Jezebel's father, Moses Carson, was a rancher. He had a ranch on the eastern end of Galveston Island, where he had around five hundred head of cattle.

"There are a lot of cattle on the island," Jezebel explained.

She and Fargo ate boiled shrimp at a little cafe within sight of the wharves. All the tables were outside, and Fargo could hear the gulls shrieking as they circled around, hoping for a handout. The breeze from the Gulf was cool, and Fargo liked the smell of the salty air.

"The eastern end of the island is still wild," Jezebel went on. "Nothing there but ranches and rattlesnakes. The ranchers don't get along too well with some of the townspeople."

"And that's why your father couldn't leave," Fargo guessed.

"That's why. Some funny things have been happening. There's a man named Jed Gunn who's been trying to buy the ranch, but of course my father won't sell. Now cattle have started to die for no reason that we can figure. My father thinks they've been poisoned somehow, and he blames Gunn. He's been keeping a close watch on things, so naturally he couldn't leave."

"How many cattle have died?"

"Enough so that we could lose the ranch. That's why we need the treasure."

Fargo threw a shrimp tail into the air, and a diving gull grabbed it before it had started back down. The gull flew away, chased by most of the others in the area, all of whom seemed to be hoping he'd drop it or that they could take it from him. Gulls weren't so different from people, Fargo thought.

"Why don't you and your father just join your uncle on the plantation?" he asked.

"It barely supports his own family. He has a wife and three sons with families of their own. So he gave us the map instead."

"And you think this Jed Gunn might not want you to find the treasure," Fargo said. "That's really why you needed me, isn't it? You want help here on the island."

"That's mostly true," Jezebel said. "Hawkins and Powell were supposed to help out with that part of things, but they changed their minds somewhere along the trail."

While she was talking, Fargo's eyes roved over the people who walked along the street. One of them was taller than the others, though all Fargo could see of him was his floppy hat. The hat looked familiar, and Fargo stood up for a better look. As he did, the hat disappeared around a corner.

"Stay here," Fargo told Jezebel.

He got up and walked away from the table. His long legs gave him a loping stride that carried him rapidly down the walk. He bumped passersby without thinking, and though some of them looked after him, nobody said a word to him. He was an unusual sight, wearing buckskins and a Colt in a town where most people didn't go armed, and they could tell he wasn't a man to trifle with.

He found that he couldn't make much progress on the walk, so he stepped into the oyster-shell street, his boot heels crunching as he walked. He kept close to the walk to avoid the buggies, and he went rapidly past the well-kept buildings with their wrought iron decoration. Some of them were three stories tall, but Fargo wasn't impressed. He'd seen trees that were a lot taller. What he wanted to see was the man in the floppy hat. That hat looked awfully familiar. It was exactly like the one Gar Bollen had been wearing.

When Fargo finally got a glimpse of the fleeing man, it was almost as if the man knew he'd been spotted. He ducked into an alley, and when Fargo got to the alley entrance, there was no sign of him.

Fargo pulled his Colt and stepped into the darker shade of the alley. It wasn't paved with shell as the street had been, and Fargo's heels sank into soft, damp earth. Fargo could smell garbage and other things less pleasant. The backs of the buildings weren't nearly as well kept as their fronts. A rat slithered across the dirt and behind a decaying wooden box that might have held apples at one time.

As he eased along the alley, Fargo heard excited shouting from one of the buildings and something smashed heavily into a back door nearby.

Fargo stepped up and jerked the door open. A heavyset woman tumbled backward, nearly knocking him back into the alley. She had very blond hair, and she was wearing a dressing gown that had come open at the top. Her generous breasts shook as Fargo pushed her out of his way and went into the building.

"What the hell do you think you're doing?" she called after him.

Fargo wasn't too sure of that himself. He saw that he was in a room full of women, all of them in various stages of undress and all of them looking at him sleepily, as if it were the middle of the night instead of the middle of the afternoon.

One of them, a woman with sooty-black hair, looked at Fargo's pistol and said, "That's a mighty big gun, mister. I like a man with a big gun."

The other women laughed. Fargo said, "Did somebody come this way a minute ago?"

The woman pointed to a stairway and said, "If you're looking for that fella who just busted in here, you'll find him upstairs. But if you're looking for a little fun, well, you've come to the right place. I might even do a good-looking jasper like you for half price."

The other women laughed again, and one of them made kissing motions in Fargo's direction. He realized that he'd stumbled into a whorehouse. It wasn't much of a surprise, considering how close they were to the waterfront. Fargo figured that men who'd been at sea for a while without a woman would make this place one of their first stops when they got off their ships.

"I'm sorry to disturb you ladies," Fargo said, as he glided along the wall to the foot of the stairs, gun in hand.

They laughed when he called them *ladies*, but their eyes were on his pistol.

"You don't need that thing in here," the blonde woman said, coming up behind Fargo. "I don't allow firearms in my place of business."

Fargo ignored her. He looked up the stairs and saw no one at the top.

"We usually charge anybody who goes up there, but we had to make an exception for your friend," the redhead said. "He was in a powerful hurry."

"He's not my friend," Fargo said. "You know him?"

"Never saw him before. But I can tell you that he's no gentleman. He threw me against that door like I was nothing but a sack of feed."

As she spoke, Fargo saw a movement at the top of the stairs. He pushed the woman away just before a bullet tore a chunk out of the banister near where she'd been standing. Fargo fired off a shot in return, but Bollen—Fargo was sure now that the man was Bollen—had already ducked back out of sight, floppy hat and all.

"Excuse me, ladies," Fargo said, putting a hand to his hat brim.

He ran up the stairs, ready to shoot if Bollen came in sight, but when Fargo got to the top there was no one to be seen. The door to one of the rooms was open, and Fargo eased down to it. He threw a quick glance inside and saw cheap curtains blowing in the open window.

Moving to the window, Fargo saw that outside it was a narrow balcony with a wrought iron railing. He looked around the window frame and saw Bollen running across the roof of the building next door.

Fargo went out the window and followed the balcony. On the wall of the next building there was a rusty iron ladder, which Fargo then climbed. When he stuck his head over the top of the roof, a bullet buzzed by him and struck the whorehouse, cracking a brick and whining away. Chips of brick spattered against Fargo's arm and side.

Fargo ducked below the roof and waited a couple of seconds before looking up again. This time there was no shot. Bollen was on the run, moving across another roof, and Fargo pulled himself up to go after him.

There was a chimney on the third building, and Bollen

ducked behind it. Fargo figured he knew what was coming, so he flattened himself against the roof.

Sure enough, Bollen looked around the chimney, his pistol ready. Fargo fired first, and the bullet took a bite of Bollen's floppy hat.

Bollen got off a quick shot that dug a trench in the roof ten feet to Fargo's left. Then he disappeared behind the chimney again. Fargo didn't move, waiting for him to reappear. When he didn't, Fargo realized that Bollen was most likely on the run, keeping the chimney between himself and the Trailsman.

Fargo got to his feet and ran to the chimney. He looked around it and saw Bollen going over the back side of the building. His head disappeared before Fargo could shoot.

When he got to the place where Bollen had dropped out of sight, Fargo saw that there was another ladder, this one going down to the alley. Bollen was just leaving the alley for the street, and Fargo went down the ladder after him.

Fargo got to the street just in time to see Bollen jump to the side of a buggy, grab the driver's arm, and throw the driver to the ground.

Not wanting to shoot on the crowded street, Fargo holstered the Colt and watched as Bollen popped the reins, urging the horse into a run. The buggy careened down the street, sending up puffs of white dust from the oyster shells and scattering pedestrians to both sides. A couple of dogs chased after it for a block or so, barking and having a high old time, but they gave up when it turned a corner on two wheels and disappeared.

There was a buzz of talk and excitement all around, and the buggy's owner was the center of attention as he brushed off his clothes and cussed the man who'd stolen his rig.

Fargo stood there for a minute and watched, then started back to where he'd left Jezebel.

He wondered what Bollen was doing in Galveston. And he realized that he still hadn't looked the man straight in the eyes.

7

"What was that all about?" Jezebel asked when Fargo sat back down at the table.

"I thought I saw someone I knew," Fargo said.

"Who?"

Fargo told her. Jezebel looked worried. She said, "He must have been looking for us."

"There's no reason for him to think we'd be here. Anyway, if he was looking for us, he's found us. We'll just have to see how the hand plays out. Right now, I think we'd better get to that ranch of yours and have a look at your map."

Jezebel stood up. "All right. Let's go."

They walked past the whorehouse on the way to a livery stable. The blond madam was leaning out a window, and she gave Fargo a friendly wave. Fargo touched his hat brim politely as they passed.

"You know Flora?" Jezebel asked.

"I make friends everywhere I go," Fargo said.

"You do get around, don't you."

Fargo grinned. "You might say that."

The livery stable smelled of hay and horses, a good familiar atmosphere to go with the other aromas that filled the island air, smells of salt and the sea, of decaying fish and dead crabs. Jezebel seemed to know the stable owner. They talked for a few minutes, and then the man walked away.

"He's going to hitch up the horse and wagon I left here," Jezebel explained. "Do you want to ride along the beach on the way to the ranch?"

Fargo thought that sounded like a fine idea. He'd seen the

flat bay waters, but he wanted to see some foam-topped waves rolling in on the shore.

Jezebel drove the wagon with a good touch on the reins, and the horse seemed to know where he was going. He didn't need any urging to head in the direction of home.

The waves that Fargo saw weren't big ones, but they were satisfactory, foaming onto the beach and making little rainbows on the dark sand. They rolled in a steady rhythm that Fargo could hear and almost feel. Little birds skittered along the edge of the greenish water, pecking at things the waves brought in, things Fargo couldn't see. There was a line of dry seaweed far up on the beach, and a boy was walking along looking for shells. The horizon was a long way off.

"Did you ever wonder what's out there, Fargo?" Jezebel asked.

"Nothing to wonder about," he answered. "It's water."

"I mean beyond the water. There are other islands out there, big ones, and way on past them is Europe."

"I never wanted to go to any of those places," Fargo said. "I've traveled a lot in this country, and it's plenty big enough for me."

"I'm not sure it's big enough for me," Jezebel said.

They drove on, and it wasn't long before they'd left the town behind. The landscape on the island side changed to one of thick bushes and low, twisted trees. There were sand dunes, too, some of them covered in green vines that crawled around and over them. Fargo could see cattle grazing on the grass among the trees.

"Not too many people come down this way," Jezebel said after they'd gone about a mile. "How would you like to go for a quick swim?"

Fargo looked back the way they had come. He hadn't seen a single person since they'd left the town behind, and there was no one on their trail. He'd half expected to see Gar Bollen lurking along after them, but the area seemed completely deserted—that was, if you didn't count the cows and the seagulls.

"You don't think anybody will bother us?" he asked.

"Not likely. Our ranch is another three miles from here, and folks from town don't come out this way."

"I guess I could do with a swim, then, as long as my modesty won't be compromised."

"You don't have to worry about that. I don't want anyone else to see you. I want you all to myself."

Jezebel drove the wagon in among the sand dunes, and set the brake. She jumped down and began to strip off her clothes. Fargo liked a woman who didn't waste time, and he joined her on the sand. Their clothes were soon removed, and, as he had every time he'd seen her naked, Fargo admired the lush curves of Jezebel's body. She put the whores in Flora's establishment to shame.

When she was undressed, she rummaged around under the seat of the wagon and came up with an old horse blanket that she spread on the sand.

She smoothed it out and then lay back on it and let Fargo enjoy looking at her firm breasts, her slim waist, the black bush at the junction of her thighs.

"When you get tired of staring," she said, "you might want to come down here. I can see that you want to."

"I don't think I'd get tired of staring," Fargo said, but he dropped to the blanket and began kissing the stiff nipples of each breast, feeling them grow even harder as his tongue teased their tips.

After he'd lathered each breast, he began working his way downward, paying special attention to the sweet curve of her navel. Her fingers tangled in his hair, and she pushed his head lower. He felt the curls of her bush brush his cheek and he knew what she wanted. He let his tongue roam freely around her nether lips with only an occasional flick at her pleasure center, teasing her until she became more insistent that he pay attention to it. She held his head in place, then began to moan and sigh and move her hips in a sinuous motion. It wasn't long before she cried out sharply and clutched Fargo to her.

After a moment she relaxed and raised Fargo's head. They sat up, and she began rubbing his rampant pole with gentle strokes. But she stopped when she noticed a scar on Fargo's forearm.

"Where did that come from?" she asked, tracing it with her finger.

"Got it from a grizzly bear," Fargo said. "I don't think he liked me much."

It wasn't the only battle scar on Fargo's body, not by a long shot, but it was the most prominent, and Jezebel wasn't the first woman to question him about it.

"Does the bear have any scars?" Jezebel asked.

"No," Fargo said.

"You mean he got the better of you?"

"No," Fargo told her. "I mean he's dead."

"I should have known," Jezebel said. She looked at the wound on his shoulder. "How does that feel?"

"It doesn't bother me if I don't think about it."

"You'll think about it if we go in that saltwater."

"That's all right. It'll probably do the wound good. It's practically healed."

"All right," Jezebel said, and she resumed her stroking.

Soon her motions got faster and faster, and all the time she watched Fargo with eager eyes. After a while, it was all he could do to hold back. That seemed to be what Jezebel had been waiting for.

"I want you inside me now," she said. "Hurry."

She lay back on the blanket and grasped his iron-hard member to guide him. He didn't need any help. Her portal was open wide, and it was slickly wet. As soon as the tip of his rod touched it, he plunged into her up to his full length.

"Ohhhh," she said.

She locked her legs behind his back, her heels digging into his rear, and held him there in a tight embrace.

"Don't move," she said. "Just let me feel you."

Fargo held still for a while. He could feel her inner muscles clasping and unclasping him. Then she began to move her hips, and Fargo joined in the motion, withdrawing almost all of the way, then thrusting full-length into her. With each thrust he saw her eyes grow wider as her pleasure increased. She was moving fast now, thrusting with him, giving as good as she got. It was almost like riding a bucking horse, and Fargo was afraid she might throw him. He could feel his climax beginning to build up within him.

"Don't hold back!" Jezebel said. "Give it to me! Fill me up!"

41

Fargo gave it to her, his climax starting at his toes and roaring up his body and out in a volcanic stream.

"Yessssssssss!" Jezebel cried. "Yesssssss!"

She quivered beneath him as she was wracked with sensual delight. Fargo did not withdraw and quickly grew hard again. When Jezebel recovered, he began thrusting, but this time with slow, languorous strokes. Jezebel seemed surprised at first, but then she joined in, helping him draw out each thrust for as long as possible and sending ripples of sensation up and down the length of his still-hard shaft.

Jezebel seemed to be enjoying it as much as Fargo, but soon she was unable to hold back, and her thrusting gained speed. Fargo was ready for her, and they rocked back and forth on the blanket until they both exploded in spasms of pleasure.

Fargo relaxed and rolled over on his back, looking up at the tall clouds that passed across the light blue sky. He heard the gulls calling on the shore and the sound of the waves washing the beach. And he heard the sound of Jezebel breathing beside him on the blanket.

He got up and took a glance at his shoulder. The wound was red and scabby, and he hoped the salt in the water wouldn't hurt it. He didn't think it would. He walked around the dune. The sand was so hot that it seemed to be burning his feet, and after a couple of steps he found himself running. The sand was deep and soft and seemed almost to pull at him.

Near the surf, the sand was damp and firm. The water swirled onto the shore and receded. It lapped around Fargo's ankles, warm as blood, and he waded out farther into the surf. When he was out almost waist deep, Jezebel joined him. She pressed herself to his back so that her cushiony breasts flattened against him.

They stood that way for a minute and then Jezebel threw herself backward, dragging Fargo under the water with her. He came up sputtering and feeling the sting in his shoulder, though it wasn't as bad as he'd expected. Jezebel swam away, laughing, slick as a fish.

Fargo swam after her, feeling the tug of the waves, but he couldn't catch her. His shoulder wasn't up to it, and besides, Jezebel had a lot more practice at swimming in the surf than he did. It was almost as if she were as at home in the water as she was on the land.

They swam like that for a while, Jezebel in the lead, Fargo trailing after. His shoulder wasn't bothering him at all, but he couldn't get up any speed. Finally Jezebel stopped and relaxed in the water, bobbing up and down on the waves. Fargo tried to do the same, but it wasn't easy for him. He kept sinking, and the waves washed over his head.

"It takes practice," Jezebel said. "But you can do it."

"I'll have to practice some other time," Fargo told her. "We need to get on to the ranch."

They emerged from the surf, and the wind felt almost cold on Fargo's wet body. Jezebel ran up the beach, her breasts bouncing. Fargo watched admiringly, then went to get his own clothes. He might not know exactly what was going on, he thought, but he was surely enjoying the sights.

8

The ranch house was made of rough rocks and it was almost completely overgrown by trees. Someone who didn't know exactly where it was might ride along the wagon track and never even see it. Fargo's eyes were keener than most, however, and he spotted it while they were still some distance away.

"I didn't think you'd see it," Jezebel said. "It's pretty well hidden."

"I guess that can be an advantage," Fargo said.

"It can if you're not overly fond of your neighbors."

Fargo said that he hadn't noticed any neighbors.

"That's the way my father likes it," Jezebel told him.

There were cows grazing not far away, and everything seemed excessively green to Fargo.

"It rains a lot here, I guess," he said.

"Pretty often, even during the summer," Jezebel said.

She drove the wagon near the front of the house and pulled on the reins. The horses stopped, and Jezebel said, "Here we are."

Fargo hopped down and they went to a porch so overgrown with vines that they practically had to move them aside to get to the door. Jezebel opened the door and called out for her father.

Moses Carson limped out of a back room. He was shorter than his daughter and tilted a little to his right. His face was covered by an unkempt beard. His shirt and pants had seen better days many years ago.

"Hello, daughter," he said. He gave Fargo a look. "Who the hell is this?"

"Fargo," the Trailsman said. "Skye Fargo."

"He's a friend," Jezebel said. "He's going to help us find the treasure."

Carson appraised Fargo with eyes half hidden in the bushy beard.

"You don't look like much," he said after a second. "Can you use that pistol?"

Fargo didn't say anything. He looked over the room they were standing in. It was furnished with a couple of chairs with cowhide bottoms, and a small table held a lamp. There were two windows, but they didn't let in much light, being nearly covered by the bushes that grew all around the house.

"He can use it," Jezebel said.

Carson looked doubtful. "Maybe he can, maybe he can't. We might just find out if Jed Gunn finds out he's helping us. You got the map?"

Jezebel took it out of her pocket and handed it to him. He unfolded it and looked it over, though Fargo didn't think he could see much in the dim light of the room.

And he couldn't.

"Let's go in the back," he said. "Where there's some light."

He turned and went through the door, and Jezebel and Fargo followed him to the back room where there was a window that was free of vegetation. The room contained a woodstove, a table, and four chairs.

Carson dragged the table over by the window, spread the map out, and bent his head over it. Fargo looked at it over the older man's shoulder. There wasn't much to see, just an outline of what Fargo assumed to be Galveston Island, with several landmarks drawn in.

"For a pirate, old Lafitte didn't make a very good map," Fargo said.

Carson's head came up. He seemed offended by Fargo's comment for some reason.

"Jean Lafitte wasn't a pirate," he said. "He was a by-God privateer. He wasn't any sea-raider. He fought under letters of marque from the Republic of New Cartegena."

Fargo recalled that Jezebel had made a similar remark, and he wondered what made them so sensitive. He said, "Doesn't matter what you call him. He was still a thief."

"Where'd you pick this son of a bitch up?" Carson asked Jezebel, who smiled and shrugged.

Carson didn't smile. He glared at Fargo and said, "Jean Lafitte never attacked a vessel under the flags of Britain or France, by God, and he was the friend of the Americans at New Orleans."

"I'll give him the credit for that," Fargo said.

"I'll just bet you will," Carson said. "You don't know a pirate from a legitimate businessman. Mighty damned ignorant if you ask me."

Fargo mulled that over for a while and then said, "Where did your brother get the money to buy that cotton plantation?"

"Nosey bastard, too," Carson said, peering at him from the thicket of hair that covered his face.

"It wouldn't be that he sailed with Lafitte, would it?" Fargo asked. "That must be it. Where else would he have gotten that much money? And why would he have had that map?"

"He might be ignorant," Jezebel said to her father, "but he's pretty smart."

"Hell, anybody with half a brain coulda figured that out," Carson said. "Shoulda figured it out before now if he had any sense at all."

Fargo went on as if he hadn't heard. "That would explain why you live out here all alone. Lafitte might have a glamorous reputation in some circles, but the aristocracy in Galveston might not think much of him."

"Ignorant bastards," Carson said, dismissing anyone who disagreed with him. "Besides, that don't have a thing to do with it. Jed Gunn wants my land and he'll do what he can to get it, even if he has to kill ever' cow I got."

"And that's why he'd try to stop you from getting the treasure," Fargo said. "Assuming it's even there in the first place."

"It's there, all right," Carson said. "My brother got this map from Jean Lafitte his own self, the night he burned Galveston to the ground and sailed off the edge of the world."

"The world's not flat," Fargo said.

Carson slammed a fist down on the table so hard that the map jumped an inch from the top.

"God dang it!" Carson said. "Don't you think I know that?

I'm not as ignorant as some people around here. It's just a manner of speaking."

"Lafitte disappeared," Jezebel said. "He was ordered to disperse his men and leave the island, so he did. But he didn't leave anything behind."

"Some of his men came back later, though," Carson said. "Like my brother. He stayed a while, and then took his money and bought that plantation. Nobody knows what happened to Lafitte, though. Hell, for all I know, he's still sailing around out there somewhere."

"It doesn't matter," said Fargo, who doubted that Lafitte was still alive. "And it doesn't matter whether he was a pirate or a privateer. All that matters is whether that map will lead you to the treasure."

"Oh, it'll do that, all right," Carson said. "If we can figure it out."

"Well," Fargo said, "why don't we give it a try."

"That's the most sensible thing you've said so far," Carson told him. "If we can trust you, that is. How do we know you ain't some kind of spy for Jed Gunn?"

"I think we can be pretty sure he's not," Jezebel said, and she went on to give her father a short version of how she'd met Fargo. She didn't fail to mention that Fargo had been wounded in saving her from Powell and Hawkins.

"Dirty bastards!" Carson said. "Put their hands on my daughter and they're dead men! It's a good thing for them I wasn't around!"

"Fargo took care of them," Jezebel said.

"Just killed one of 'em. Should've killed 'em both."

Fargo said he was sorry for doing such a shoddy job.

"Damn well should be. But I guess your heart was in the right place."

"Think we can trust him?" Jezebel asked.

"Maybe," Carson said. "We'll see."

He smoothed out the map again and said to Fargo, "Here, have a look."

He showed Fargo what some of the landmarks were, pointing them out with a wrinkled brown finger.

"This here is where Lafitte's house was. *La Maison Rouge,* he called it. 'The red house.'" He moved his finger. "Here's where the town is now, but it's not on the map, of course. And here's where the treasure is."

He put his finger on a spot marked with an *X*. It appeared to be near the beach some distance away from the town. In fact, it wasn't far from the spot in the dunes where Fargo had just spent some time with Jezebel, who hadn't mentioned that episode or any similar ones in her report to her father about what had happened.

"What are those markings right there?" Fargo asked, putting his own finger on the map next to Carson's.

"Oak trees," Carson said. "My brother told me about those. Looks like three of 'em together."

"Shouldn't they be easy to find?"

Carson gave him an exasperated look. "How long you been on the island, Fargo?"

"Less than a day."

"Well, hell, look around you. How many oak trees are there on this island?"

Fargo admitted that he hadn't counted them.

"Well, there's a damn sight more'n three."

"But these are gathered together."

"Don't make much difference. There's all kinds of triple oaks growing around."

Jezebel looked over their shoulders and said, "Doesn't it look like those trees are on some kind of hill?"

Fargo didn't know how many oak trees there were on the island, but he knew how many hills there were. None.

Carson agreed. He said, "There ain't a hill within fifty miles of here, on the island or the mainland. It can't be a hill."

"The east end of the island is higher than this end," Jezebel said.

Fargo knew that was true. The Carson ranch house was almost exactly at sea level. An especially high tide would probably come right up to the door. But the east end was at least a few feet higher.

"Don't see what difference that makes," Carson said. "There's still not a hill."

"Look at the location," Jezebel said. "Maybe it means that the three oaks are where the elevation begins to increase."

"Be hard to spot the exact place it does that," Carson said.

48

"Not if there are three oaks growing close together," Jezebel pointed out. "It's worth looking at, anyway."

Carson considered it, rubbing his hairy chin. Finally he said, "All right, we can go have a look. I'll let Ben and Billy know. We might need them to help us dig."

"Ben and Billy?" Fargo said.

"Hired hands," Carson told him. "They bunk down at the barn."

Fargo had seen the house, but he hadn't seen any barn. He asked where it was.

"You could miss it easy," Carson said. "It's off in some trees over on the other side of the island from here. Not that it's very far. I'll go fetch the boys in the wagon." He folded the map and put it in his pocket. "If we find old Lafitte's treasure, we won't have to worry about losing the land. We can build us a house in town right next door to Jed Gunn. I'll bet he'd like that."

With that, he left the kitchen, and Jezebel grinned at Fargo.

"What do you think of him?" she asked.

"He doesn't seem to have a very high opinion of me."

"Oh, yes, he does. If he hadn't liked you, he probably would've said something bad about you."

"You mean he was being kind?"

"In his own way," Jezebel said.

"Should be interesting to hear him talk to someone he doesn't like."

"Then get him started on Jed Gunn."

"Some other time," Fargo said.

9

Billy and Ben turned out to be tall and laconic, thin as oak planks, and looking just as hard. Their skin was browned by the sun and they sported mustaches stained with tobacco. They looked so much alike that Fargo thought they must be brothers, maybe even twins. The only way Fargo could tell them apart was that Ben was wearing a red bandanna around his neck, while Billy's was blue. They sat in the back of the wagon and had nothing to say as Carson drove them up the island. It was almost as if they were angry at each other, but if they were, it wasn't any of Fargo's business. It had taken Carson a while to fetch them. Maybe they'd been fighting.

Fargo sat with them and wondered where they might have come from. They looked tough enough to have been part of Lafitte's pirate crew, but they were much too young, probably not over twenty-five. Both of them had pistols in holsters strapped to their legs, and Fargo figured they knew how to use them.

Also in the wagon were a couple of shovels, which Carson had tossed in just in case they got lucky; some rope to pull the treasure chest up out of the hole, and a small keg of gunpowder on the off chance that there would have to be some blasting done. Carson had even put in a couple of lanterns to use if they had to do some digging after nightfall.

"You never know," he said. "We might find it first thing. Wouldn't that be the proper stuff? Just dig it up or blow some oak roots out of the way, and there it is, pure gold, shining like the sun."

Fargo wasn't optimistic. The map had seemed awfully vague to him. Jezebel's idea about where the oak trees were was as good as any, which meant that it wasn't very likely at all. Those trees could be just about anywhere. The map didn't even appear to be drawn to scale. Finding those trees was going to be as much a matter of luck as anything.

Besides, Fargo wasn't convinced that the map was genuine. Maybe Carson's brother had been Lafitte's trusted friend—or maybe not. And even if he had been, it could be that the old pirate—or privateer—hadn't buried anything more valuable than a keg of rum.

Fargo didn't say any of that to Carson. The old man deserved his chance to find the treasure. He was going to be disappointed enough if it wasn't where he hoped it was without having Fargo cast a dark shadow of doubt over the whole enterprise.

"First thing, we have to find the oak trees," Carson said as the wagon rolled smoothly along the sandy road. "Then we can start in to dig."

That was another problem as far as Fargo was concerned. Just where were they to dig in relation to the trees? On the east side or the west? North or south? The map didn't make it clear at all.

Ben and Billy didn't comment, either. Ben brought out a plug of tobacco from somewhere in his shirt, cut off a piece, and handed it to Billy, who took it silently, stuck it in his mouth, and began to chew. Ben then cut a piece for himself and stuck the rest back wherever it had come from.

"You shouldn't count your money before you have it," Jezebel told her father.

"Ain't counting it. Just thinking about it. By God, I'll bet Ben and Billy are, too. I could pay 'em all the back wages I owe 'em. How about it, boys?"

They were nearing the dunes where Jezebel and Fargo had dallied earlier, and Fargo never did learn what the two young men might have thought about Carson's idea because he saw the afternoon sun glint off something beside one of the dunes and before he could shout a warning, a rifle shot cracked. A round hole appeared just over the bridge of Billy's nose and tobacco spurted out of his mouth just before he flipped over the side of the wagon as if jerked backward by a rope.

Carson thrashed the reins and the horses began to run. Another shot took one of them down in mid-stride, and when it fell, the wagon turned over, tumbling the passengers out on the hot sand.

Fargo landed on the shoulder where Hawkins's bullet had struck him, and he almost cried out in pain. He rolled over twice, came up in a crouch, and grabbed Jezebel, who was a couple of feet away, looking dazed. Fargo pulled her into the shelter of the overturned wagon. Bullets thwacked into the hard wooden sides and slapped into the sand nearby.

"Keep your head down," Fargo said.

He jerked out his Colt, snapping off a couple of shots just to keep things interesting while he looked around for Ben and Carson.

Ben had rolled behind a low dune and was firing his own gun. Fargo didn't think he was hitting anything, though. Carson was lying out in the open, facedown, not moving.

Fargo holstered his pistol and ran for the old man, the sand dragging at his heels and bullets whipping by his head. He reached Carson without being hit and grabbed him under the arms. He dragged him back to the wagon, feeling as if he were moving through molasses. His wounded shoulder felt weak. A bullet tugged at his shirt. Another one took off his hat. But he got back to the wagon and laid Carson on the sand.

"Is he all right?" Jezebel asked, her face showing her concern.

Fargo didn't know. He said, "See about him."

He looked over at Ben, who was reloading, and then tried to estimate how many men they were up against. He'd counted at least three different locations where the shots were coming from, possibly a fourth.

He didn't have to wonder about who was doing the shooting. He'd had a brief glimpse of a floppy hat just before the first shot had been fired.

Gar Bollen.

What Fargo couldn't figure out was why Bollen was after him, or why he'd followed him to Galveston in the first place. Surely a little saloon fight wouldn't make Bollen mad enough to ride the vengeance trail all the way down to Galveston.

After a little thought, Fargo realized that Bollen probably hadn't followed him at all. He'd been on the island before Fargo. Maybe he'd just seen him on the street and decided to kill him. But how would he know to set up an ambush in the dunes near Carson's ranch? And why run away when he spotted him? Why not just fight it out in the street?

Fargo didn't have time to puzzle much over his questions. He was more worried about how he and the others were going to survive.

"He's all right," Jezebel said beside him.

Fargo looked over and saw that Carson was trying to sit up.

"Let go of me," he told his daughter. "I'm fine. Just got the wind knocked out of me when I fell. What the hell is going on?"

"Somebody's trying to kill us," Fargo said.

As if to emphasize his point, another round of bullets slapped the sand close by.

"The hell they are," Carson said. "If they'd wanted to kill us, we'd be dead now. They want the map."

"The only reason we're not dead is that somebody shot the horse," Fargo pointed out. "If the wagon hadn't turned over, they'd have killed all of us. They've already killed Billy. They might want the map, but they want to kill us to get it."

"The sons of bitches. If I had a gun—"

"But you don't," Jezebel said. "What are we going to do, Fargo?"

Fargo looked things over. The Gulf of Mexico was at their backs, and Gar Bollen was in front. The Gulf didn't look nearly as inviting to Fargo as it had earlier that day. Bollen had never been attractive.

Aside from the Gulf and Bollen, there was nothing to see except the sand dunes and the gulls whirling and calling overhead. And there was nowhere to go.

"What happened to that gunpowder?" he asked.

"It rolled right over there," Jezebel said, pointing behind them.

The little keg was lying about twenty yards from where they were, down toward the surf. If he went for it, Fargo would be exposing himself to gunfire again, but he couldn't think of any other chance they had.

He handed Carson the Colt and said, "Cover me."

Carson didn't ask questions. He raised up and started firing. Fargo went for the gunpowder.

Bollen and his crew must have been waiting for someone to show himself because they opened up with all they had. Carson and Ben fired back, but they weren't able to provide much distraction. Fargo was sure he'd be hit.

And he was, or at least his boot was. A bullet struck the right heel, slicing it neatly off and sending Fargo tumbling. He did an ungraceful somersault and landed a foot from the keg. He wondered how many pieces he'd separate into if a shot hit the gunpowder, but he didn't wonder long. He scooped up the keg and short-legged it back to shelter.

"This must be your lucky day," Carson said when Fargo flopped down beside him. "You don't have a scratch on you."

"Got my boot," Fargo said, setting the keg on the sand and putting out his hand for the pistol.

Carson handed it to him, and Fargo started looking for the rope that he'd seen earlier in the wagon.

It was still right there, lying by the two shovels. Fargo tied it around the middle of the keg, making the knot as tight as he could.

"What you planning to do?" Carson asked. "Heave it at 'em?"

Fargo didn't think he could have thrown the keg very far even if his shoulder had been in good shape. He said, "I'm going to let your horse take it over there to them, I hope."

"You'll play hell getting him unhitched," Carson said. "And he might not be able to walk anyway."

The dead horse had pulled the other horse down with her, and they lay on the sand at the front of the overturned wagon.

"Don't want her up yet," Fargo said. "I have to tie the rope to her first."

"They'll kill you."

"They don't want to kill me, remember? They just want the map."

Carson laughed. "You got a hell of a sense of humor, boy. Too bad you won't live long enough to use it anymore."

"You never know," Fargo said. He reloaded the Colt and handed it to Carson. "Try to hit somebody this time."

"Hell, how can I hit 'em if they won't show themselves? Cowardly bastards. If they'd fight fair—"

Fargo didn't wait to hear what Carson would do if Bollen's

boys would just fight fair. He slithered on the sand out to the horses, keeping behind them as best he could. He was hoping that Carson would keep Bollen's attention and give Fargo time to get the rope tied to the horse and then get the horse unhitched . . . and that Bollen wouldn't kill the horse.

It didn't take long, and as soon as Fargo moved away the unhurt horse struggled to her feet.

"We have to make her run into the dunes," Fargo said when he got back to cover and got his pistol back from Carson. "When she does, I'll shoot at the keg and hope there's enough of a spark to blow it up."

"What're we supposed to do if it does blow up?" Carson asked. "Run?"

"We wouldn't get anywhere," Fargo said. "We'll go after Bollen instead."

"Bollen? Who's Bollen?"

"I'll tell you later," Jezebel said.

Fargo checked his Colt, reloaded, and said, "Can you get that horse started?"

"Damn right," Carson said.

He crouched at the front of the wagon and took off his hat.

"Tell me when you're ready," he said.

Fargo took his bandanna from around his neck and tied it over his face.

"Anytime," he said.

"All right, then."

Carson started yelling, flapping his arms, and slapping his chest with his hat. The horse didn't move immediately, and Carson became even more agitated. Finally he stood up and threw his hat at the animal.

"Get out of here, you spavined scoundrel beast!" he yelled, and ducked back behind the wagon.

Fargo didn't know whether it was the hat or the yelling, but the horse got on the move.

Carson had ducked down just in time. A bullet whipped the air where his head had been.

"Sons of bitches!" Carson said, but Fargo hardly heard him. He was watching the rope, which followed after the horse, who was moving at a good pace, and the keg bounced right along, too. Fargo watched it go.

The horse was moving toward the dunes, and when she went behind the first one, Fargo got ready. Because the keg was bouncing on the sand, it was going to be a difficult shot. He wasn't going to have more than three shots. Maybe just two. He had to make the most of them.

The horse disappeared behind the dune. The keg hung for just a second on a vine, then bounced.

Fargo was ready. He shot once and hit the keg. Nothing happened. He shot again.

This time something must have caused a respectable spark because the volatile gunpowder exploded with a thunderous crash.

Sand and vines flew everywhere, spattering the wagon and flying high into the air. The gulls sheered away and flew far down the island, and a white cloud of smoke spread and rose, covering everything.

Fargo ran forward, his ears ringing as he choked on the smoke and sand even through the cloth over his mouth and nose. He hoped that he could get a shot at Bollen, though it wasn't likely. There was sand in his eyes and he could hardly see anything other than the dim outlines of the dunes.

He certainly didn't see the body he tripped over. He fell to the sand and lost his pistol. While he was trying to find it, a horse ran past him so close that he fell backward.

He looked up, expecting to see Bollen, but he didn't. He couldn't quite credit what he saw, which was a woman riding hell-bent for leather around the dune, her horse's hooves churning sand. Before he could get a good look at her, she was gone, so fast that he wondered if he'd been imagining things.

It took him several seconds to find the Colt. He tried to make sure the barrel was clear of sand and then went looking for Bollen.

He didn't find him, but he did find someone else, someone whose squat form he recognized, even from the rear.

"Powell!" Fargo said. His voice rang hollowly in his ears.

Powell, who was in the act of mounting his horse, didn't respond. He swung his leg up over the saddle and kicked the horse's flanks.

Fargo fired twice, but his vision was still obscured by the cloud of blowing smoke and sand, and he missed both times.

56

There was no chance to shoot again. After the second shot, Powell was completely out of sight.

The breeze from the Gulf began to clear away the smoke, and sand had stopped falling from the sky. Fargo pulled the bandanna from his face and wandered through the dunes looking for Bollen. He found no one, except the body he'd already stumbled upon. This time he noticed that it had no right arm, but he didn't need the arm to recognize the man as one of those who'd been with Gar Bollen in the Potters' saloon. It was the one called Willie, who had been a little too close to the keg of gunpowder when it exploded. Well, Fargo thought, Willie had hoisted his last drink.

Fargo found Willie's arm a few yards away. The hand was still clutching a pistol. Fargo bent down and removed the gun from the clenched fingers. Willie wasn't going to need it anymore.

About that time Ben showed up, closely followed by Jezebel and Carson.

"We saw Bollen ride off, and one of his men was with him," Jezebel said.

"The other one's over there," Fargo said. "It's your friend Willie."

"Dead?" Jezebel asked.

"Dead," Fargo agreed. He handed Willie's pistol to Carson. "You might want to hang onto this."

"Thanks, Fargo," Carson said. He stuck the pistol in his belt. "I'm sorry about all this. I didn't know they'd be laying for us. How the hell did they know about the map?"

"Somebody told them," Fargo said.

He knew now why Bollen was in Galveston. He hadn't come on his own.

"Who could have told them?" Jezebel asked.

"Sim Powell," Fargo told her.

"Sim? Is he here?"

"He's here, all right. I saw him. Tried to shoot him, but I missed."

"What's he doing with Gar Bollen?"

"I figure they fell in together after that little fracas in the Potters' place. Maybe Sim is the one told Bollen about the treasure."

"Bastards," Carson said. "Well, we'll be ready for 'em the next time."

"Maybe," Fargo said.

He hoped there was no more to it than that, but he thought there might be. He said, "There was someone else with them."

"Who?" Jezebel asked.

"I don't know. I never saw her before."

"Her?" Carson asked. "You telling me there was a woman doing some of that shooting?"

"I couldn't see her very well, but I think so."

Jezebel looked at her father. "Amanda Gunn. It couldn't be anybody else."

"Son of a bitch," Carson said.

10

They righted the wagon and laid Billy's body in it, wrapping him in the same blanket that Fargo and Jezebel had used earlier that day for a far different purpose.

"He'd want a proper burial," Carson said, "with some reading from the Book. And he'd want to be buried on the place."

Ben spit tobacco on the sand and nodded agreement.

"What about the horse?" Fargo asked. "We can't pull this wagon back to your house."

"If I know that horse, she's running yet," Carson said. "She might stop when she gets to the end of the island, or she might not. If she does, she'll come home tonight."

"What about Willie?" Fargo asked. "You want to bury him?"

"Hell, no. I'd rather bury the horse that the bastards shot. But we'd better do both. We got the shovels. We'll bury the horse first."

The gunpowder had created a hole deep enough to hold a horse, so they decided to take advantage of it. It took all four of them to drag the horse into it using a rope they'd tied around the body. Fargo was hampered by his missing boot heel, but they managed. After the burying was done, he wasn't at all sure they'd accomplished much. Carson told him that it would be all right.

"Critters'll come out of the water and eat most of her, sooner or later," he said. "Now let's take care of that Willie fella."

It was easy enough to dig a shallow grave in the sand and roll Willie's body into it.

"Don't forget the arm," Ben said. It was the first sentence

Fargo had heard him speak. "A man deserves to go to glory with both his arms. Don't matter what kind of man he was."

Fargo fetched the arm and threw in the open grave. It landed on Willie's chest and stayed there.

"Close enough," Ben said, and they covered Willie over with wet sand as the sun was going down in the West, coloring the sky with vivid streaks of orange and red.

Carson leaned on his shovel and said, "I never thought I'd be digging a grave today instead of digging for treasure. And Billy dead in the bargain. That bastard Jed Gunn has a lot to answer for."

"What about Amanda Gunn?" Fargo asked. "Tell me about her."

Carson looked out toward the Gulf.

"I don't like the look of that sky," he said, and sniffed the air. "Don't like the smell, either."

Fargo couldn't tell any difference from the way things had looked and smelled earlier, and he said so.

"That's because you've never lived on this island," Jezebel said. "My father's lived here for a long time. He can read the weather signs."

"I hope I'm wrong," Carson said. "But I'd say a big blow might be heading our way in a day or so."

"Hurricane," Jezebel explained for Fargo's benefit.

"Maybe not, though," Carson said. "They strike all up and down the coast. Might not be coming in here. Might not be coming at all."

Fargo hoped not. He'd never experienced a hurricane, and he was pretty sure he didn't want to.

"You're forgetting about Amanda Gunn," he said.

"I ain't forgetting anybody. She's Jed Gunn's sister, and she's meaner'n a rattler with a sore tail. I'm not surprised she was out here trying to kill us. She'd do it just for the hell of it and not think twice about it. She's even worse than her damn brother."

"Why do they know about the treasure map in the first place?" Fargo asked. "It seems to me you'd keep a thing like that a secret."

Carson looked toward the slowly sinking sun and said, "It's gonna be dark before you know it. We'd better head on back to the house. We can come back and get the wagon in the morning."

Just then Fargo looked at the dunes and saw something big and dark moving through them.

"Maybe we won't have to," he said. "Isn't that your horse coming back?"

"By God, it is," Carson said. "Still dragging that rope, too. She must've run east toward town, and now she's started back home. Go fetch her, Ben."

Ben walked away without comment, which was how he did most things.

Fargo said to Jezebel, "If I didn't know better, I'd think your father spends as much time not answering my questions as he does answering them."

Jezebel laughed. "He's like that. Especially when the answer might embarrass him."

"I'm not embarrassed," Carson said. "Hell, everybody knows I talk too much sometimes. I guess I might've bragged to Jed Gunn that he'd never be able to get my land and that I had a way of getting my hands on more money than his thieving daddy ever did. I don't remember doing it, but I could've."

"So you told him about the map."

"I sure as hell don't remember doing that. It's been a family secret for a long time. But when I get mad, I don't always know what I'm saying. My mouth just seems to work all by itself."

"Did he know Jezebel was going after the map?"

"He knew she was leaving town. You can't keep something like that a secret in a place like this."

Fargo was beginning to get a picture of things that was a little different from the one he'd had only minutes before.

"Where did you meet Sim Powell?" he asked Jezebel.

She thought it over and said, "It was right after I left my uncle's place. He and Hawkins met me on the trail and told me how dangerous it was for a woman to travel alone. I had the map with me, so—wait a minute. Are you thinking that Jed Gunn sent them after me?"

"I wouldn't be surprised, not if Gunn's as bad as you say."

"Hell," Carson said, "He's worse. Why that son of a bitch would—"

"Never mind," Fargo said. "That must be what happened. Powell and Hawkins decided to string Jezebel along for a while, make sure she had the map, find out where it was hidden, and then have a little fun with her before bringing the map back to Gunn."

"I should never have told them about the map," Jezebel said.

"They may have known already," Fargo reminded her. "So don't feel too bad about it."

"I feel bad because now that Hawkins is dead, Powell's got Bollen with him to help out."

"Bollen doesn't look to me like the helping kind," Fargo said. "I'd say he's taken over."

"Don't nobody take over from the Gunns," Carson said. "This Bollen must be working for them."

"Maybe we'll find out," Fargo said, still not satisfied that he had the straight story on why things had turned out as they had.

Ben led the horse up to them, holding firmly to the rope. The horse's eyes were still a little wild, and she was obviously skittish.

"We can rig something up," Carson said, "and she can pull us home. Then we'll have to decide what to do next."

"Next I'm going to find my boot heel," Fargo said.

He went back to the beach and followed his tracks to where the keg had lain. The boot heel, or what was left of it, was lying on the sand. Fargo picked it up. He thought he might be able to nail it back on the boot, and it would be better than nothing.

"Now that you got it, why don't we go see about taking care of Billy," Carson said.

"I'm ready," Fargo said.

They drove back to the ranch through the deepening twilight, and the lightning bugs came out to flicker through the grass and bushes. When they reached the house, Carson said, "I'll go in and get the Bible."

The others sat in the wagon and waited. No one felt like talking.

Carson came out holding a worn, leather-bound volume

and climbed back up on the wagon seat. He said, "Take him down where we buried Ruth."

"My mother," Jezebel said to Fargo, and clucked to the horse, who had calmed down considerably.

There was a big oak tree near Carson's barn, so old that the lower branches spread out for what seemed to Fargo to be twenty feet or more.

Fargo and Ben dug the hole as deep as they could without it flooding with water. Not deep enough, Fargo thought, but it was the best they could do. They laid Billy in it, still wrapped in the blanket, and Carson repeated the Bible verses about the Valley of the Shadow of Death.

The shadow under the tree was dark and deep, and only a few stars sparkled in the cloudy night sky. Fargo knew that Carson couldn't see the words in the book he held open in his hands. He was reciting them from memory.

When he was finished, Ben said, "Amen," and he and Fargo shoveled dirt and sand over the body.

"Now, then," Carson said, "Billy was a good man, and he's been killed by those bastard Gunns. Are we gonna let 'em get away with it?"

"He was my brother," Ben said, confirming Fargo's earlier suspicion. "I guess I have to do something."

"What can we do?" Jezebel asked.

"Fix my boot," Fargo said.

"While you're doing that, we'll rustle up something to eat," Carson said. "And then we'll see about those damn Gunns."

Supper was beans, bread, and bacon, with strong coffee to drink. During the meal, Carson cussed the Gunns, while the others listened. Finally, he said, "We can't let 'em get away with trying to kill us. I'm going into town to face 'em."

"You can't prove they did anything," Jezebel said. "We're not sure who it was, except for Sim Powell."

"Fargo saw Amanda."

"We don't know that. He just thinks he saw a woman. He's never met Amanda."

"I don't care, by God. It had to have been her, and I'm gonna pay 'em a little visit."

He shoved his chair back from the table and stood up.

"Then I'm going with you. Fargo, will you come?"

Fargo shrugged. He wasn't enthusiastic about the idea, but he'd developed a liking for Carson and didn't want to see anything happen to the old man. He said, "I guess I'll go along for the ride."

"Ben?" Jezebel said.

"I'll go," he said. "I better go down to the barn and get my pistol."

"Might be a good idea," Fargo said, and Ben left the kitchen.

"Let's load up the wagon," Carson said.

He went out of the room, not looking back to see if Fargo and Jezebel were following.

They hadn't unhitched the horse from the wagon, so it was ready to go. Carson and Jezebel got up into the seat. After a while, Ben joined them and he and Fargo climbed into the back. Jezebel drove them away.

11

The trip to Galveston in the dark was interesting to Fargo because he'd never ridden past the Gulf at night before. Low in the sky, the moon was coming up full and bright, and now and then the clouds would blow away from it and let it shine down on the water. The pale light made a silvery path on the surf, narrow at the horizon and getting wider as it approached the shore. The sound of the waves washing the sand was as persistent as ever, and the wind blew steadily across their tops.

When they reached the town, Fargo was impressed with the large houses, all of which sat up two or three feet off the ground.

"So the water can go under them if there's a storm," Jezebel said when he asked. "That way, they won't be flooded."

Fargo didn't like talk about storms. He'd heard more than enough about that sort of thing already.

Many of the houses had walled gardens, and Fargo could see the tops of flowering bushes showing over the walls and rustling in the breeze from the Gulf. Most houses had wide porches, and all of them had windows on all sides to catch the wind from the Gulf and let it blow through on the humid summer days. Most of the streets and some of the houses were even illuminated by gas lighting.

"Almost like daylight after dark," Carson said.

It wasn't that bright, Fargo thought, but it was a lot different from being on the open plains under a sky full of stars. Not any prettier, just different.

They rode slowly down a street lined with trees, their branches reaching out over the wagon, and Carson said, "That's the Gunn house right down there."

The largest house that Fargo had seen yet stood on the corner. The yard was full of flowering plants, and there were buggies and buckboards parked all along the street.

"Looks like the Gunns are having themselves a party," Carson said.

"Maybe we'd better just drive on by," Jezebel said. "This doesn't look like a good time to be accusing them of anything."

"Good a time as any," Carson said. "I don't care who hears what I have to say."

Jezebel sighed as if resigned to her father's impulses. She pulled back on the reins and the wagon came to a stop in the middle of the street.

"You all can stay here if you want to," Carson said. "I'm going to the party."

He climbed out of the wagon, and Fargo watched him walk away. When he was almost to the gate in the picket fence that fronted the Gunns' yard, Jezebel said, "Well? Are we going to sit here, or are we going with him?"

She got down without waiting for an answer. Ben looked at Fargo, who said, "We might as well go. We don't want to miss the fun."

Ben spit tobacco over the side of the wagon and got up.

"Guess not," Fargo said.

The house was full of people, and some of them had spilled out onto the porch and into the yard. They were dressed in evening clothes and gowns and all of them were laughing, talking, and drinking from crystal glasses brought to them by servants dressed in red livery with gold trim. The women were wearing white gloves. Somewhere inside the house a piano was playing a song Fargo didn't know.

No one seemed to notice when Carson opened the gate, but when Jezebel, Ben, and Fargo arrived, people began to look up and whisper among themselves. Fargo wasn't surprised. He must've looked pretty strange in his buckskins, and the others were all dressed in rough ranch clothes. They didn't look much like anybody else at the party.

People fell silent as Carson walked up the steps and onto the porch. He called out Jed Gunn's name and waited.

After a few seconds, a man worked his way through the

crowd and came through the front door. He was tall, with wavy chestnut-colored hair, a high forehead, and dark eyes. He had a blocky face that contrasted oddly with his full, soft-lipped mouth. His shirt was stiff with starch and so white that it seemed to shine with a light of its own.

"I don't believe your name is on the guest list," he said to Carson. He looked over Carson's head and out to the street. "And those ruffians you brought with you weren't invited, either."

"One of those ruffians is my daughter," Carson said.

"Oh." Gunn nodded. "The way she's dressed, it's hard to tell. My apologies."

"I don't give a damn about your apologies. I want to know why your sister tried to kill me this afternoon."

A murmur went through the guests at that remark. Fargo thought that most of them had probably never heard anybody be so rude to a man like Gunn. Not in public, anyway. There was probably plenty of rudeness in Gunn's world when there wasn't a crowd around.

Gunn's soft lips thinned and hardened. "I don't allow that kind of talk in my house. Not from anyone."

The music inside the house came to a stop. Some of the guests were starting to look a little excited to Fargo. They probably thought something was about to happen.

And they were right.

Carson's hand went to his belt, and he pulled out the pistol that Fargo had taken from Willie's body, aiming it at Gunn's stomach.

Gunn didn't appear bothered. He said, "You don't need that, Carson. You wouldn't shoot me in my own house."

"The hell I wouldn't. You had your men ambush me this afternoon, and they killed Billy Sloan."

Gunn seemed surprised. He said, "I'm sorry to hear about Mr. Sloan, but you must be mistaken about my having any part in it. I don't even know what you're talking about."

"The hell you say."

Jezebel nudged Fargo with her elbow.

"Do something," she said.

Fargo figured that Carson was doing all right by himself, but he pushed the gate open and stepped through. The guests watched him as he strode along, a tall stranger in outlandish clothing. He hadn't quite reached the porch when a woman came out the front door.

She was wearing a green gown that revealed her white, lightly-freckled shoulders and a whole lot more. Her long red hair fell below her shoulders, and her green eyes matched the gown.

"What's going on out here?" she asked.

Gunn looked at her and smiled.

"Hello, Amanda," he said. "Mr. Carson seems to have the idea that we tried to kill him this afternoon."

"That's ridiculous," Amanda said. "Send him away."

"You heard her," Gunn said. "I think it's time for you to go. You're interrupting her birthday celebration."

Fargo went up on the porch and stood beside Carson.

"I think I saw you earlier today," he said to Amanda.

She was much shorter than he was, and she looked up into his eyes

"I don't believe so," she said. "I'm sure I'd remember a man like you."

There was something in her tone that implied a lot more than she actually stated. Fargo smiled. He wouldn't mind seeing what she looked like without that dress, not that she didn't look plenty nice with it on. Her breasts swelled up over the top of it. They were small, but they were high and proud.

"You probably would," he told her with a grin.

She turned to her brother and said, "Have you been introduced to this man?"

"No," Gunn said, not looking pleased with the question.

"Then someone should do the honors," Amanda said. "Mr. Carson?"

"This here is Skye Fargo," Carson said.

He looked down at the pistol he was holding and stuck it back in his belt.

Gunn didn't offer to shake hands, and neither did Fargo. Amanda was another matter.

"I'm pleased to meet you, Mr. Fargo," she said, giving a brief curtsy, bending just enough to let him see still more of her breasts, which were freckled across the top like her shoulders.

"I'm pleased to meet you, too," Fargo said. "And your brother."

Gunn just looked at him. It was clear that he wasn't pleased to meet Fargo or to have Carson standing there on his porch.

Fargo didn't care. He didn't much like Gunn, either. He said, "I've enjoyed your party, Miss Gunn, and I hope you have a nice celebration. But now I think it's time for us to get on back where we came from."

"Are you sure?" Amanda asked. "You might enjoy the party even more if you stayed a while."

"Some other time," Fargo said.

Amanda smiled. "Let me know when."

Her brother's face was getting red, but Fargo wasn't sure just who Gunn was mad at. He decided it didn't matter. He touched Carson's shoulder and said, "Time to leave."

The old man sighed. "I guess you're right. I shoulda known he'd never admit being a back-shooting bastard."

He had turned and taken about half a step when Gunn reached out a hand, grabbed his shoulder, and spun him around.

"Nobody talks to me like that," he said, and slammed his fist into the middle of Carson's face.

Carson staggered back. He grabbed for Fargo's arm and got hold of the elbow. When he fell down the steps, he dragged Fargo with him, and they landed in a heap in front of a man and woman who stared down at them as if they were some kind of rare animals.

Fargo untangled himself from Carson and was getting to his feet when Jezebel ran past him. She went up the steps, planted herself in front of Gunn, and slapped his face.

"You bastard," she said coldly.

Gunn gave her a speculative look and rubbed the side of his face with his hand.

"You should be ashamed of yourself, hitting a defenseless old man," Jezebel continued.

From her brother's side, Amanda said, "Maybe somebody should hit *you*."

The two women made an odd pair, Fargo thought as he helped Carson stand up. Amanda was short and fiery, while

Jezebel was tall and icily calm, but they were both quite pretty in their own way.

"Why don't you try it," Jezebel suggested.

Amanda pulled up her skirts and kicked Jezebel in the knee. Jezebel slumped forward in surprise. When her head went down, Amanda clipped her on the point of the chin with a small balled fist, and Jezebel tumbled down the steps.

Fargo and Carson tried to catch her when she got to the bottom, but they got in each other's way. She fell into their arms, and all three of them collapsed to the ground. There was a lot of laughter from the party guests, and Fargo thought they were getting a lot more entertainment than they'd counted on.

It took a little longer for Carson and Fargo to get untangled this time, but Jezebel finally separated herself from them and all three stood up. Fargo dusted himself off, but Jezebel went charging right back up the steps. Carson reached out to stop her, but he was too late. She was already on the way.

Amanda had her back turned and was saying something to her brother when Jezebel plowed into her. They disappeared through the doorway and into the house. Fargo heard the sound of glass breaking, and Gunn rushed inside to see what was happening. When he did, Carson took off for the steps.

A couple of the party crowd who must have wanted to get in on the fun grabbed Carson and pulled him back. He stomped on the toe of one, who yelled and released him, allowing Carson to pull the pistol and point it at the other.

The man let go of him at once, putting his hands in the air and backing away. But two other men jumped on Carson from behind, knocking him to the ground. Carson cried out, but he kept his grip on the gun.

Fargo was about to help Carson get out from under the men when he heard a scream from inside the house. He figured that Jezebel needed his help more than her father did. He ran up the steps.

He crossed the porch and looked through the door. Jezebel and Amanda were lying on the hardwood floor amid shards of broken glasses that had fallen from a tray carried by one of the slaves when the two of them ran into him. He was standing helplessly by, as was Jed Gunn, who didn't seem to know what to do to help his sister.

At first glance, it didn't appear to Fargo that Amanda needed any help. She was sitting astride Jezebel, her hands buried in the larger woman's hair. She was methodically beating Jezebel's head against the floor.

Then Fargo saw that Jezebel had her hands around Amanda's throat. Amanda's face was turning dark, but she didn't stop pounding Jezebel's head.

Fargo reached out, grabbed Amanda's long red hair, and jerked her backward. Jezebel was strong, but Fargo was stronger, and he tore the screaming woman from Jezebel's grip, pulling her to a standing position beside her brother.

Amanda wasn't as grateful as Fargo thought she should have been. When he released her hair, she whirled on him, kicking his shin repeatedly. Her face was dark red, redder than her hair, but Fargo figured it was red with anger rather than lack of breath.

He shoved her aside and started to help Jezebel get up. Something hit him in the back of the neck, and instead of helping Jezebel, he fell squarely on top of her.

By now the whole house and yard were in an uproar. Fargo could hear the noise echoing off the walls. Then something hit him again, and he got mad. He didn't mind an honest fight, but having someone hit him while his back was turned and then hit him again while he was down struck him as cheating.

He shoved a struggling Jezebel across the slick floor and stood up, his boots almost skidding on the hardwood. He saw Jed Gunn with his arm drawn back, about to hit him in the back again. Fargo didn't give him a chance. He hit him in the softness of his mouth.

Blood burst from Gunn's lips, and he staggered back into the arms of several of his surprised friends, who threw him right back at Fargo. Fargo hit him in the stomach three times very fast, then clubbed him in the side of the head with the heel of his fist.

Gunn's eyes rolled up in his head, and he went down as if he'd been shot.

Fargo didn't have time to admire his handiwork. Amanda jumped on his back, wrapped her legs around him, and began clawing at his face.

Fargo peeled her hands away, but he couldn't shake her off his back. Her legs gripped him like iron bands.

He heard Jezebel yelling and felt himself being dragged backward. He knew that Jezebel was trying to do something about Amanda, maybe pull her off his back, but it wasn't working. If anything Amanda was clinging to him even tighter.

"Let her go!" Fargo said, and the pulling stopped.

Fargo looked around to find a wall that wasn't covered with furniture. When he saw one, he turned and backed into it as hard as he could.

All the air whooshed out of Amanda, and she went limp. Fargo moved away from the wall and let her slide to the floor, where she lay gasping and looking at him with something that seemed more like respect than anger. There even seemed to be a slight smile on her lips.

Gunn lay not far away. Two men were kneeling beside him. One of them was bathing his face with a wet cloth. His eyelids fluttered, but Fargo didn't much care if he came to or not.

Jezebel stepped to Fargo's side and said, "Let's get out of here."

"Good idea," Fargo said.

And then the shooting started.

12

Fargo went to the door and shoved a couple of men aside. He saw that Moses Carson was firing his pistol into the air, yelling and hopping around at the same time. People were scrambling to get away from him.

Someone pushed past Fargo, and he saw that it was Jezebel, who was on her way to help her father.

"Hold on," Fargo said. "I think he's doing all right."

They stood and watched until Carson calmed down. After a few seconds he stood still and looked at the people standing at a respectful distance from him.

"That's better," he said. "I'll teach you to gang up on a Carson. The next time one of you sons of bitches puts a hand on me, I'll shoot it off."

He glanced up at the porch and saw Fargo and Jezebel.

"You two can come on down," he said. "I think I've got everybody calmed down out here. What about those damn Gunns?"

"They're inside," Fargo said. "I don't think they'll mind if we leave."

"Well, let's light a shuck, then."

Fargo and Jezebel walked down the steps and joined Carson. They all stood in the yard for a moment. The party guests were very quiet.

"I have a feeling we won't get invited to the Gunns' next birthday celebration," Jezebel said with a laugh.

"Or the one after that, either," Carson said. "But I sure as hell had fun at this one, didn't you?"

"I've had more fun from time to time," Fargo said. "Where's Ben?"

"Out there," Carson said, pointing to the street.

Ben was waiting for them outside the gate. When they got there, he said, "I tried to get in and help, but it was too crowded. They kept pushing me back out here."

"Don't worry about it," Carson said as they walked back to the wagon. "We didn't need any help. It was the Gunns that needed it. We did just fine by ourselves. I expect the Gunns'll think twice before they mess with us again."

It sounded good, but Fargo reminded Carson that he was forgetting something.

"They didn't have Bollen and Powell to back them up tonight," he said. "It might've been different if they had."

"I'm not worried about those two," Carson said.

That sounded good, too. But Fargo didn't think it was realistic. Bollen and Powell were the kind of men that it paid to worry about.

They all got into the wagon. Jezebel released the brake and clucked to the horse, who pulled them down the street past the house.

Jed Gunn stood on the porch, watching them, holding a red-stained handkerchief to his swollen mouth. Judging by the look in Gunn's eyes, Fargo thought that if Gunn had been armed, he would have shot them all.

Amanda was standing beside him, and she looked even more murderous than her brother. But when her eyes met Fargo's, he thought he saw something besides hate there, something that looked an awful lot like an invitation. He thought it might be a good idea to see if he could meet Amanda again sometime soon. Maybe he could find out if she had freckles all over her body, or just on her shoulders and chest.

"We'll look for the treasure again tomorrow," Carson said. "They won't bother us again."

Fargo wondered if Carson really believed that.

Fargo didn't. Not for a minute.

There was no room for Fargo in the house. He knew that Jezebel would gladly have shared her bed with him, but her father wouldn't have approved, and Fargo didn't want to make the old man mad. So he bunked with Ben, who was silent as ever.

74

Fargo was curious about a couple of things, however, so he decided to see if he could find out the answer to a question or two. He said, "Billy looked a lot like you. Was he your twin?"

"No," Ben said. "He was a year older."

He didn't seem inclined to say more, but Fargo went on.

"You didn't seem too upset when he got killed, so I was just wondering."

"Upset?" Ben said. "I guess not. We were brothers, but that's about as far as it goes. We didn't get along all that well."

Fargo would have asked if there had been a falling out but he figured it was none of his business. Anyway, his curiosity was satisfied for the time being. If he wanted to know more, maybe Jezebel or Carson could tell him.

He went to sleep and dreamed about pirate gold and red-haired women.

The next morning got off to a bad start when Ben came into the kitchen and announced that two more cows had died.

"Poisoned," Carson said. "Gunn's work, no doubt about it. That's where those bastards that waylaid us were last night, out killing my cattle. All right, let's go have a look at 'em."

Fargo wasn't interested in poisoned cattle. He had something else in mind. He said, "While you do that, I'm going to ride up the island and have a look around. Maybe I'll spot those three oak trees."

"Good idea," Carson said. "If you find 'em, come back and get us. You want to go with him, Jezebel?"

Fargo hoped she would say no, and she did.

"I think I'll stay here," she said with a look around the kitchen. "This place could use some cleaning. I don't think you and Ben have been paying much attention to it while I've been gone."

"You can take Billy's horse, then," Carson told Fargo. "Ben won't mind, will you, Ben?"

Ben didn't even seem interested. He said, "Nope."

"Thanks," Fargo said.

As he rode the big dun that had until recently belonged to Billy Sloan down the beach, Fargo noticed that the roar of the surf seemed much louder than it had the previous day. The wind was from the northeast, and the sky far out over the Gulf was an odd color, a sort of dusty red.

He rode past the spot where the attack had occurred, and he saw the mound where the horse was buried. It was covered with scuttling creatures, and Fargo knew that there were probably others down under the sand. He wondered if they were feeding on Willie, too. Not that it mattered.

As he got closer to the town, he saw more and more people out on the shore. Nobody was bathing in the Gulf. Everyone was looking out at the sky and the surf.

He stopped, slid out of the saddle, and walked over to a couple standing on the beach with a large dog. The dog wasn't worried about the weather. He charged out into the water, swam for a few strokes, then ran back out on the beach and shook himself from nose to tail, sending a shower of water droplets flying everywhere.

"Funny looking sky," Fargo said.

The man and woman looked at him.

"You from around here?" the man asked.

He was tall and thin and had a fringe of beard around his chin. The woman was shorter, with a plain face and a thin-lipped mouth.

"Just visiting," Fargo said.

"That's what I figured. If you'd been from here, you'd know that sky doesn't look good. It means we might have a storm coming. 'It will be foul weather today, for the sky is red and lowering.' Book of Matthew."

"Don't borrow trouble," Fargo said. "For things might turn out better than you think. Book of Fargo."

The man gave Fargo a puzzled look.

"I don't believe I'm familiar with that book," he said.

"Wouldn't expect you to be."

Fargo touched his hat brim and went back to his horse. If people wanted to believe that the color of the sky could tell them what kind of weather they were going have, that was all right with him. But he didn't put much stock in that kind of sign. There were some things in nature you could rely on: geese returning to the North in springtime, for one. But the color of the sky over the water? He didn't see what that had to do with anything.

He looked overhead. The clouds were big and puffy and moving fast. Their flat bottoms were black, but the tops were white as cotton. They didn't look like storm clouds to him. But he'd decided that he didn't like islands. He preferred places that had as many ways out as there were coming in. He liked places that stood up higher than the surrounding water. The way he figured it, there wasn't a place on the whole of Galveston island that was more than ten feet higher than the surf.

Thinking about that, and about the houses built up off the ground, Fargo turned his eyes to the Gulf again. It seemed to him that the water was a good bit higher up on the beach than it had been yesterday. In fact, it seemed just a little higher up on the beach than it had been just a few minutes before.

Just the tide, he told himself. A high tide would naturally come up a lot farther than the water would be at low tide. Yesterday, he'd seen the water at low tide, and today it was high.

That would have been a comforting thought if he'd really believed it, but he couldn't quite convince himself it was true.

When he arrived at the residential area, he saw that some of the smaller houses had whitewashed clapboard walls. He hadn't noticed, at night, how very white they were. When the clouds allowed the sun to shine though, the walls were so white that Fargo had to squint to look at them.

There were no whitewashed houses near the Gunn mansion, for that was what it was. Fargo could see that now. It was two stories high, and it sat on a lot more ground than he had previously realized. There were no buggies parked in front this morning, but Fargo knew better than to go up to the front door of a house like that. They'd gotten away with it last night because of the party that had been going on, but daylight was an entirely different matter. There would be a servant on duty, and Fargo wouldn't get past him without using force.

So Fargo rode around to the back of the house. There was an alleyway of hard-packed dirt, and the stone wall that concealed the garden in front ran all along the back of the property. In the middle of the wall there was a wooden gate.

Fargo dismounted and tied the reins to the ring on a short hitching post by the gate. The hitching post was probably there for the convenience of merchants who made deliveries to the Gunns, he thought.

There was no lock on the gate and it squealed when Fargo pushed it open. In the damp and salty Gulf air things rusted and corroded quickly.

Inside the gate there was a flagstone walk, and off to one side was a small house that Fargo figured for the slave quarters. He followed the walk to the back porch, mounted the steps, and knocked on the door.

The knock was answered by a thin black man whom Fargo recognized. He'd been carrying the tray of glasses that had been broken at the party.

"Yes?" the man said.

It was clear from his tone that he recognized Fargo, too, and that he didn't much like seeing him there.

"I'm here to see Miss Amanda," Fargo told him.

The man looked at Fargo steadily, without speaking. It took Fargo a second or two to catch on. When he did, he removed his hat and held it in his hands in front of his belt buckle.

"Who shall I say is calling?" the man asked when the hat was removed.

"Fargo. Skye Fargo."

The man turned and left Fargo standing there, hat in hand. Fargo was uncomfortable. He didn't like being made to feel like a beggar, but he figured the man who'd greeted him knew all about how that felt. He didn't begrudge him the chance to get a little dignity back.

After what seemed like a long time, the man returned. He said, "Miss Amanda says she doesn't know anyone named Skye Fargo."

Fargo sighed and held onto his temper.

"Just tell her we met last night," he said. "I think she'll remember."

The man went away again. Fargo held his hat by the brim and turned it around and around in his hands.

Finally, the man returned. He opened the door and said with evident distaste, "Miss Amanda will see you in the parlor."

Fargo followed him through the kitchen and into a hall. There was a doorway on the right, and they went through it. Amanda Gunn was sitting in a high-backed chair reading a thick leather-bound book. Or pretending to read. Fargo wasn't sure.

She looked up when the two men entered the room and dismissed the servant.

"I believe we could use some fresh vegetables for dinner tonight, Isaiah," she told him. "Why don't you go to the market and buy some. Don't get anything that Jed doesn't like."

"Yes, ma'am," Isaiah said, plainly unhappy with the order. He wasn't smiling when he left the room.

When he was gone, Amanda closed the book she was holding and laid it on an end table.

"Shakespeare," she said, tapping the book with one short finger. "I find his works most enlightening. Do you read, Mr. Fargo?"

"I can read, if that's what you mean. I can even read Shakespeare if there's an occasion to. But I don't find the time too often."

"I'm sorry to hear it. I think reading is what gives a man culture."

"I'm cultured enough to come here to apologize for what happened last night," Fargo said.

Amanda's eyes widened in pretended surprise.

"Why, I'd forgotten all about that," she said.

"I hope I didn't hurt you too much."

"Hurt me? How could you have done that? By trying to crush me to death? Is that it?"

"I'm in truly sorry I had to do that. You were about to claw my eyes out."

Amanda laughed. "I was, wasn't I? You really shouldn't have hit my brother, Mr. Fargo. Jed and I stick up for each other."

"So I noticed."

"That is perhaps our only good quality," Amanda said. "Sticking up for each other, I mean. In fact, it's a good thing for you that Jed's not here. He's not as forgiving as I am."

Fargo didn't doubt her. He said, "I don't know about your brother, but I think you probably have some other good qualities."

"Why, Mr. Fargo. Whatever do you mean?"

"I think you know," he said.

"Perhaps I do. Would you like to see more of the house?"

Fargo had seen enough of the house, but something in the way she said it caught his attention.

"If it wouldn't be too much trouble," he said.

"Oh, no trouble at all. There are some quite interesting rooms. Up on the second floor."

She stood up. She was just as short as Fargo remembered, and her hair was just as red. Today she was wearing a modest dress that covered her figure, but the soft swell of her breasts was visible beneath the cloth, and Fargo thought about those freckles.

"What kind of interesting rooms do you have upstairs?" he asked.

Amanda smiled. "The bedrooms," she said.

"Isaiah often takes quite a while to do the marketing," Amanda told Fargo as they went up the stairs. "And his wife, Lucinda, is cleaning their quarters today. She won't be in until it's time to cook lunch. That will be an hour or so yet."

Amanda wasn't leaving much doubt about what her intentions were. Fargo felt his manhood stirring in his pants.

When they reached the top of the stairs, she took his hand and led him to a room at the end of the hall. She opened the door and stood aside to let him look inside.

There was a canopy bed, a nightstand that held a bowl and basin, and a single chair. Against one wall there was a dresser with a tall mirror. Sunlight came in through two high windows open to catch the breeze.

"I like to sit in front of the mirror and brush my hair," Amanda said. "I like to do it when I'm naked. What do you think of that?"

"I think I'd like to see you brush your hair," Fargo said.

Amanda gave him a wicked grin.

"And so you shall," she said.

She pulled him inside the room and closed the door.

"When?" Fargo asked.

"Right now," she said.

"Let's have a look outside first," Fargo said, walking over to the window.

She came to stand beside him, and he pointed out the color of the sky.

"Ever see it like that before?" he asked.

"Never. You don't believe those old sayings about the color of the sky, do you?"

"I never used to," Fargo said. "But this is the first time I've ever seen a sky like that."

"I'll show you something else you've never seen before," Amanda said, and she began to remove her clothes.

13

Her dress and underthings had more hooks, buttons, pins, and stays than Fargo had ever seen, yet she was out of her clothing and naked as an eel in what seemed like mere seconds. She stood brazenly before him, hands on her hips, her legs apart, and said, "Well, Mr. Fargo?"

"Well, what?" he asked.

She put her hands over her head and twirled around on her toes until she was facing him again.

"Well, have you ever seen anything like it before?"

She was small and perfectly proportioned. Her breasts, instead of being large and billowy like Jezebel's, were small as apples and just as firm, tipped with pert, dark nipples. Her stomach was flat, and the crisp curls at the junction of her thighs were a golden red. There were no freckles below her breasts.

"I may have seen something like it," Fargo said, "but I've never seen anything I liked better."

"My, my, you certainly do talk sweet for a man with all his clothes on. Why don't you get them off while I brush my hair?"

She walked over and sat on a stool in front of the dresser. There was a hairbrush on a mirrored tray, and she took the brush in her hand. Watching Fargo in the mirror, she began to brush her hair with long, practiced strokes.

Fargo's tool was standing at attention before he got his clothes off, and he could see Amanda eyeing it with approval in the mirror. When he was naked, she put the brush back where it had lain and turned around on the stool.

"You look ready for some fun," she said. "And so am I."

She stood up and walked over to Fargo. She put her arms around him and pressed herself to him.

"I like feeling you against me," she said.

Fargo had to admit that he liked the feeling, too. Her skin was as warm as a winter fire.

After a moment Amanda pulled away and said, "Come to the bed."

Fargo followed her, noticing the tight muscles of her rear as she swayed across the floor. When they reached the bed, she took his hand and turned him around. Then she pushed him back on the bed. Before he quite knew what was happening, she was straddling his chest. He could feel the slick wetness of her as she slid herself up and down.

She touched the nearly-healed wound on his shoulder with her fingertips.

"What happened to you?"

"I got shot," Fargo said.

That seemed to excite Amanda even more, and she rubbed herself against him again. Then she lifted his hands to her breasts and placed the palms on the stiff nipples. He kneaded both breasts, and Amanda threw back her head, gasping in pleasure.

"I like being on top," she said, after a moment. "What do you think?"

Fargo thought she was the kind of woman who always had to be in control, and if he let her get the better of him now, she would always think she had the upper hand. He didn't want her to think like that.

So he removed his palms from her breasts and put his hands under her arms. Then he stood up. She hardly seemed to weigh anything at all.

"What are you doing?" she said.

"This," Fargo told her, and threw her onto the soft bed.

While she was thrashing around, he stepped to the dresser and picked up the hairbrush. He went back to the bed and sat on the side. Then he grabbed Amanda around the waist with one hand and pulled her across his lap.

"You bastard!" she said, seeing the brush. "If you dare lay a hand on me—"

"I don't plan on using my hand," Fargo said, giving her a light smack on the rump with the brush.

"Oh!" she said, kicking her legs furiously. "Don't you dare do that again."

Fargo did it again, noting that the brush hardly left a mark because he was wielding it so gently.

Amanda pretended to be hurt. She beat on the side of the bed with her fists and cried out.

"If you touch me again with that brush, my brother will kill you!"

Fargo gave her another light smack, then started to toss the brush away.

"Oh," Amanda said. "Don't. Every time you touch me with it, I feel it somewhere else."

"Where?" Fargo asked.

"You know."

Fargo said he didn't.

"Down there," Amanda said.

"Oh," Fargo said, giving her another light smack.

"Yes," she said. "Yes."

He turned the brush over and rubbed the bristles against her firm cheeks.

"Ah. Ah. Ah," she said. "Please, Fargo. Please."

"Please, what?"

"Please, put the brush down and take me. Now! Hurry!"

Fargo tossed the brush on the floor and turned Amanda over on the bed. She writhed on the bed, her eyes closed, her bottom lip caught in her teeth. Her short but shapely legs scissored the air.

Fargo plunged between them and the tip of his pole found the right spot as if it had been guided by an unseen hand. She was hot and buttery and ready for him, and he slipped inside her with ease.

As soon as he entered her, Amanda sank her fingernails into his back and began thrusting her hips at him eagerly. Fargo met her eagerness with equal desire and short, quick strokes that got longer and harder until he was afraid he might send her flying off the bed.

As if aware of his thoughts, Amanda tightened her grip

with her hands and locked her legs around him. Her breath came in rapid gasps as she urged him on.

"Faster, damn you, faster!" she cried.

Suddenly she stopped moving altogether. Fargo wondered if she had fainted, but then her entire body began to spasm.

"Ohhhhhhh!" she cried. "Oh! My! God!"

Her orgasm racked her like an earthquake, and her inner muscles clamped around Fargo's manhood, causing him to release waves of pleasure. When he thought he was done, she clasped him again and again, bringing his climax to a higher level each time.

When it was over, they lay on the bed, as tired as if they had run for miles, but much more satisfied. Fargo had never felt so drained.

But he hadn't come there to make love.

Well, that wasn't true. He'd known, maybe even hoped, that Amanda wanted him, and he had certainly wanted her. She was a beautiful woman, and it was only natural for him to be attracted to her.

But she was also the woman he'd seen riding with Gar Bollen, or he thought she was. She'd already denied it once, but he'd planned to ask her about that.

Now seemed like as good a time as any.

"I think I saw you yesterday," he said.

The feather-filled mattress was soft and yielding. Amanda turned slightly and rolled into Fargo's side.

"I know you did," she said, trailing her fingers down his chest. "At the party."

"Before that," he said.

"Before that? I don't see how that could be possible."

"I told you before. It was down at the beach. You were with Gar Bollen?"

"Gar Bollen? Is that a man or a fish?"

There was no hesitation, no indication in her tone that she might be lying. She was good, very good, Fargo thought.

"He's a man," Fargo said. "I thought you might know him."

"I'm afraid not."

Her hand strayed to Fargo's relaxed manhood and began stroking it. Before long, it wasn't relaxed any more.

"He works with a man named Sim Powell," Fargo said, his voice only a little strained.

"I never heard of him, either. Are you sure they're from Galveston?"

"Oh, they're not from Galveston?" Fargo said. "Maybe they work for your brother."

"That's possible. I don't know everyone who works for Jed." She moved her hand in a certain way. "Do you like that?"

"Yes," Fargo said.

She moved her hand again.

"And that?"

Fargo caught his breath.

"Yes," he said.

"Then I expect you'll really like this."

Fargo really liked it. He turned to her and started sucking the tips of her breasts, first one, then the other. He sucked harder and harder, until it was Amanda who was catching her breath.

"That's almost as good as the hairbrush," she said. "Don't stop."

Fargo didn't stop. He worked his tongue over the erect nipples and moved his hands down Amanda's back to her smooth rear end to begin squeezing the cheeks.

"Ah," Amanda said, spreading her legs. "I'm ready, Fargo. Ride me."

Fargo was ready, too. He entered her again, and this time was just as frenzied as the first. If anything, Amanda was even more shaken by her explosion at its conclusion.

It took both of them longer to recover this time. Amanda was the first to speak.

"Does that big cow of a Carson woman do the things for you that I do?"

"Not exactly," Fargo said.

"I don't see how a woman of that size could ever satisfy a man. There's just too much of her."

That was a matter of opinion, Fargo thought, and an uninformed opinion at that. He'd found that women of all shapes and sizes provided their own unique pleasures. But there was no need to tell Amanda that.

"She's ugly, too," Amanda said. "Don't you think so?"

"There's all kinds of beauty," Fargo said.

Amanda sniffed. "There's also no accounting for taste, not even bad taste."

Fargo hadn't come there to discuss Jezebel. It was time to change the subject. He said, "Why does your brother want the Carsons' land?"

Amanda regarded him suspiciously.

"Who said he wanted it?"

"Moses Carson."

"That old man. He's crazy. Everyone knows that. Living down there on the wild end of the island, raising cows. No one wants his land."

"Someone's killing his cattle," Fargo said.

"And I suppose he told you *that*, too."

"Yes."

"Even if my brother did want the land, which isn't the case, he wouldn't stoop to poisoning cattle. He's not that kind of man."

"What kind of man is he?"

"The good kind," Amanda said. "The kind who wouldn't understand at all if he came home and found you here. And speaking of that, I believe it's time for you to leave."

She rolled off the bed and began gathering up her clothing.

"I enjoyed your visit," she said. "I hope you'll come again sometime."

Fargo looked at her and grinned.

"I'll try do to that," he said.

14

When Fargo rode out of the alley on the dun, he encountered Isaiah, who had his hands filled with the groceries Amanda had sent him for. Isaiah stood to one side and let Fargo pass. He gave the Trailsman a look filled with pure hate, and Fargo wondered what the relationship between him and Amanda might be. Fargo didn't know whether Isaiah was a slave or a freeman, but whatever the relationship between the mistress and the servant was, it was bound to be complicated.

Fargo continued riding on into town. The wind seemed a bit stronger to him and everywhere he looked people were boarding up windows and bringing things from their yards into their houses. Fargo didn't like the implications, and he turned the dun's head toward the beach.

The sound of the surf was much louder than it had been, and the waves were crashing instead of making a steady sound. The water was up much higher than it had been earlier. In fact, there wasn't really any beach left to speak of, just a thin sliver of sand. It didn't look good, but Fargo didn't see any other signs of a storm. The sky was still an odd color, not reddish so much as a sort of sickly yellow out over the Gulf, but that didn't mean much to Fargo.

People lined the beach now, looking out toward the horizon as if they might be able to see the storm coming, if indeed it was on the way. Fargo didn't stop to talk. He had other things to do.

Fargo spent the rest of the morning and most of the afternoon doing what he'd told the Carsons he was going to do: looking around for the three oak trees.

It was true that there were oak trees all over the island, and often there were three of them together. Sometimes there were four or five. There were houses where oak trees grew in the yards, and there were oak trees along the streets.

Fargo had never thought much about trees before. They were there, or they weren't. He could distinguish different kinds, but it wasn't something he gave any special importance to. Now it was beginning to seem that there was an oak tree everywhere he looked. But the group of trees that looked most promising was the one that Carson had been heading for the previous evening. It grew not far from where the ambush had been staged, and it seemed to Fargo that the trunks of the three trees must have been twisted together when they were small, causing the three trees to look like one giant oak.

After looking this unusual growth over, Fargo rode back to the wharves and ate oysters and boiled shrimp with tangy red sauce at the outdoor cafe where he and Jezebel had eaten the previous day. He was the only customer, and while he was sitting there, Flora, the madam from the whorehouse he'd stumbled into, walked by. Other than a few slaves on errands, there was no one else on the street, and Fargo gave her a wave. She smiled and came over to his table.

"You don't mind being seen with me?" she asked.

She was wearing a fancy dress and carrying a parasol that she didn't need. The wind was about to turn it inside out. She wore a hat that covered most of her blond hair. The wind was worrying the hat, too, but it somehow stayed in place. Fargo wondered how many pins she'd anchored it with.

"I never minded being seen with a lady," Fargo said. "Besides, if you'll look around, you'll see there's hardly anybody to notice us. I think everyone is too worried about the storm to come outside. Maybe it's too windy for them. Sit down, and I'll buy you a drink."

"There was never a man bought a whore a drink unless he wanted something from her," Flora said, but she pulled out a chair and sat in it.

Fargo waved for the anxious-looking waiter and asked Flora what she wanted.

"Beer," she said, and Fargo said he'd have one, too.

"Think there's going to be a storm?" Fargo asked while they waited for their beer.

"Could be," Flora said. "Wouldn't be the first one here on the island. Hasn't ever been a bad one, though, not yet. When the bad one comes, I hope I'm not around for it. This whole island will be under water."

Fargo was of the opinion that any storm was a bad one when you were trapped on an island that sat as low in the water as the one they were on. Even a high tide could cover it.

The waiter brought the glasses of beer and put them on the table.

"Will you be staying much longer?" he asked.

"Why?" Fargo asked.

"Because we're going to close, and we're going to take all the tables inside."

"We won't be long," Fargo said, and the waiter went away. But he didn't go far. He stood in the doorway, watching, as if he was ready to snatch up the glasses as soon as they were empty and carry them inside to safety.

Flora took a drink of her beer and wiped her mouth with the back of her hand.

"Not bad for the first one of the day," she said. "You raised quite a ruckus in my place yesterday. What was that all about?"

"I wanted to talk to the man I was chasing," Fargo said.

"Must've wanted to talk to him pretty bad. I saw you yesterday with that Carson girl. You know the Carsons?"

"I know them," Fargo said. "Do you?"

Flora laughed. "They wouldn't have much to do with the likes of me. I know those boys that work for them, though, Ben and Billy. They come by the house now and then. For a while there, they were pretty regular. I hear that somebody killed Billy last night. That's too bad. He was a good customer. Never got rowdy or tried to make the girls do things they didn't want to. Not like that friend of yours."

Fargo had been wondering if he was going to get anything for the price of the beer. Now he thought he might.

"What friend?"

"The one you were chasing. He came back by last night. I guess he liked what he saw."

"And he caused trouble?"

"Nobody causes trouble in my place," Flora said. "But he

tried. He cut one of my girls. Star. Some men need things like that, but I don't allow it. I heard Star screaming, and got out the shotgun. When he saw that, he left. He didn't want to, but nobody argues with a shotgun." Flora paused. "I should've killed him, I guess, but there'd be too much explaining."

Fargo was sorry she hadn't pulled the trigger. He didn't think anybody would miss Gar Bollen.

"Was there anyone with him?" he asked.

"Not that I saw."

Fargo wondered where Powell might have been, not that it mattered.

"Billy and Ben came together, though," he said.

"Yes. They were always polite. That's the kind of customers I like."

"Billy didn't get along very well with his brother, though," Fargo said.

Flora had another drink. "Well, that was because of that woman, that Jezebel. They gave her the right name when she was born, that's for sure."

"You're telling me that Ben and Billy had a falling out over Jezebel?"

"That's right. That's why the two of them came to my place now and then. They were both in love with her, but she wasn't interested in either one of them. So they had to find some relief. That kind of thing happens all the time, and I'm glad it does. It's good for business."

"Jezebel doesn't strike me as the cold type," Fargo said, trying not to sound as if he was speaking from experience.

"Oh, she likes men well enough. Better than most, from what I've heard. But she just didn't like those two."

"Who did she like?" Fargo asked.

Flora drained the beer glass and set it on the table. The waiter was there instantly. He grabbed it and looked at Fargo.

"Are you through?" he asked.

Fargo wasn't, but he didn't really want the beer. He said, "Take the glass and tell me the damages."

The waiter told him and Fargo paid. But he didn't leave the table. He stood there, looking at them expectantly.

"I think he wants us to leave," Flora said.

"What gave you that idea?" Fargo asked.

Flora laughed. "I can generally tell when a man's tired of me. And I need to be getting back to the girls."

She stood up, and so did Fargo. The waiter grabbed their glasses and went inside with them.

Fargo said to Flora, "I'll walk you to the house."

"Are you sure? It won't do your reputation any good."

"I'm not even sure I have a reputation around here," Fargo said. "And it wouldn't matter, anyway. Besides, I wanted to ask you another question or two."

"I should have known," Flora said. "But I don't mind. I always like the company of a good-looking man. So you can come along if you want to."

They walked away with as much dignity as the wind would allow them. After a few steps, Flora finally gave up on the parasol, folding it and tucking it beneath her arm.

"I don't much like the feel of this weather," she said.

Fargo didn't like it either. But he told himself that high wind and high water didn't mean that there would be a storm. Even if there was a storm, it might not come to Galveston. It might strike the shore somewhere miles away.

"You never answered my question about who Jezebel liked," he said.

"I thought that would be obvious to you," Flora said. "She liked Jed Gunn. I expect she still does."

"I don't know about that," Fargo said. "But you could be right."

He thought about it. Amanda had seemed to have an intense dislike for Jezebel, and Fargo should have known it hadn't begun at last night's party. Amanda might very well be jealous of Jezebel because of her relationship with Jed, whatever it had been. However, as far as Fargo knew there was no relationship now.

"What came between Jezebel and Gunn?" he asked.

"Her father," Flora said. "He's not a part of the island society, any more than I am. He's a rancher and not a very big one at that. Besides, the story goes that some of his family was associated with Jean Lafitte, that pirate that used to live here. Most people don't want a pirate in the family. But the funny thing is, none of that ever bothered Jed Gunn. He would have married Jezebel in a minute if she'd have had him. And she would have. But her father wouldn't stand for it."

Fargo wondered if that explained why Gunn was so eager to get his hands on Carson's property. If Gunn owned the ranch, Carson might let Jezebel marry him just in hopes of getting it back.

"The old man's just too proud," Flora continued. "He thinks that the island society would snub his daughter if she married Jed, and he's probably right. I don't think that would bother Jed, though."

"You seem to know quite a bit about Jed," Fargo said.

Flora looked at him and smiled.

"I know a lot of men," she said. "One way or another. They talk to me and the girls about things they wouldn't say to anyone else, because we're good listeners. Being a whore isn't all about a quick poke for money, you know."

Fargo said he was glad to hear it, and then they were in front of Flora's place of business.

"Would you like to come in?" she asked. "The girls were all interested in you."

"I'd better not," Fargo told her. "I need to get back to the Carson place before the water gets any higher."

"You never did tell me what you were doing with the Carsons," Flora said.

"That's right," Fargo said.

"Is it Jezebel?"

"Let's just say I'm a friend of the family."

"That's good enough for me," Flora said. "I hope you don't get caught in the storm."

"Thanks," Fargo said.

Flora went up the steps, turned, and waved good-bye to Fargo before she entered the door.

Fargo walked back to where the dun was tied, wondering about all she'd told him, trying to make it fit with everything that had happened. He couldn't quite work it out, but he didn't let it bother him. Sooner or later everything would make sense.

It almost always did.

15

As Fargo rode out of town, the sky darkened and the wind blew harder, whipping the fringe of his buckskins. He turned the dun's head toward the beach, and when he got there he saw waves higher than any he'd seen before. They were crashing onto the sand with increasing force, and the beach had disappeared completely. If this kept up, Fargo thought, the water would soon be running through the streets of Galveston.

There was no one other than Fargo to see the spectacle. Apparently people had seen all they cared to and had gone to seek shelter. Fargo thought they'd had the right idea, and he headed down the island for Carson's ranch.

On the way, he passed near the three oaks that had been twisted into one, and he decided to have another look at them. Before he got to them, however, he saw movement. Not knowing who might be there but curious to find out, he stopped behind a dune and dismounted. He dropped the reins to the ground, hoping the big horse was trained well enough to stay there, and slipped around the dune for a better look.

There were three men working with shovels at the foot of the oak trees. The noise made by the wind and the surf was so loud that Fargo couldn't hear the men talking, though he could see that they were. He couldn't even hear the sounds their shovels made as they cut into the sand.

Even without hearing them, however, Fargo thought he had a pretty good idea of who they were and what they were digging for, and when he saw Gar Bollen's floppy hat and beard, he was sure.

One of the men looked up and glanced in Fargo's direction. Fargo slipped behind the dune, but the horse wasn't there. It had ambled off around the other side and was headed toward the oak trees.

Although the horse was saddled, a dead giveaway that there had been a rider, Fargo wasn't too worried. He couldn't go after the animal, but because of the unusual weather, Bollen and the others might think that it had thrown its rider and wandered away.

Things didn't work out that way, though.

Fargo waited a while before he sneaked a look. When he did, he saw the horse standing about halfway between the oak trees and the dune where he was hiding, but the men were nowhere in sight.

Fargo's hand went to the butt of the Colt, but it was too late. Someone standing behind him said, "Don't do it, Fargo. Just ease that hand on down."

It was one of Bollen's men, the one called Joe. Fargo did what he was told, not having any great desire to be shot in the back.

"Stand easy," Joe said, speaking loudly so that he could be heard over the roaring of the wind and the Gulf. "Don't try anything."

Fargo stood easy, and Bollen and Sim Powell came strolling around the dune, their pistols leveled at him. Joe reached out, slipped the Colt out, and stuck it in his belt. Then he stepped back.

"I knew we'd be meeting again, Fargo," Bollen said. "Sooner or later."

The wind whipped at the brim of his hat and flipped it up so that Fargo could finally see his eyes. They were dark and sunk back in his head, which made it appear that Bollen was staring out of a cave. But there was a light in the eyes, and Fargo thought it was the light of madness, the kind of madness that led a man to do whatever he felt like at any moment: rob, kill, burn—it didn't matter to a man with eyes like that.

"I can't say I was looking forward to it," Fargo told him.

"Can't say that I was, either," Bollen said. "Sim, though, Sim's mighty happy you're here. Ain't that right, Sim?"

"That's right," Sim said. "Can I kill the son of a bitch now?"

Bollen laughed. It was about as nasty a sound as Fargo had heard in a while.

"No, you can't kill him now."

"He spoiled my fun with the Carson woman," Sim said. "And he killed Lute."

"I don't give a damn about Lute," Bollen said. "I never even met him. I don't give a damn about your fun, either."

"He killed your partner, too," Sim said.

"Yeah, he did. Not that I give a damn about Willie."

Sim looked puzzled as if he didn't understand what kind of man he'd thrown in with.

Fargo could have told him. He'd known men like Bollen before. All they cared about was themselves. Back at Potter's salon, Bollen had said he'd get Fargo, but it wasn't for what Fargo had done to Bollen's men. It was the insult to Bollen that mattered.

Fargo didn't try to tell Sim any of that. He thought it would be better if Sim figured it out for himself. Assuming Bollen didn't kill Sim for the fun of it before he had time to think it over.

And considering the kind of man Bollen was, Fargo decided to see how far he could be pushed.

"Cut any women lately, Bollen?" he asked.

Bollen's mad eyes narrowed. Then he smiled a thin smile.

"Been consortin' with whores, Fargo?" he asked.

Fargo didn't answer, but Bollen didn't seem to mind.

"What do you think, Joe?" Bollen asked. "Should we kill Fargo?"

"Hell, no," Joe said. "If we kill him, he can't dig for us."

Bollen nodded his approval.

"See, Sim? Joe's a thinking man. If Fargo does the digging, we don't have to. And even if he don't find a thing, we don't care, do we?"

Sim still hadn't figured things out. He said, "Why don't we?"

"Because he'll have saved us the trouble of digging him a grave," Bollen said. "That's why."

"So we *are* going to kill him?"

"That's right. We're going to kill him. But not now. First he'll have to do a little work for us. Then we'll kill him."

"Can I do it?" Sim asked.

"We'll see," Bollen said. "I might want to do it myself, considering his mouthy ways." He smiled the thin smile again. "Or maybe I won't kill him. Maybe I'll just shoot him in the knee and kick him in the hole. Then you can cover him up. You can watch the sand while it covers his eyes and fills up his mouth. How'd that be?"

"I guess that'd be all right," Sim said. "But it's a hard way to die, even for him."

"That's what's good about it," Bollen said. "Come on, Fargo. Let's see how your hand fits one of those shovels over there."

Fargo didn't move.

Bollen laughed and said, "You got guts, Fargo, but it won't do you any good. You're gonna dig or die."

"I'm going to die anyway, remember?"

"Right. But you're gonna dig first."

"Why should I?"

"Because if you don't, I'll shoot your toes off one at a time, and then I'll start on your fingers."

Fargo shrugged. He might as well dig. You never could tell what might happen. Maybe he'd find the treasure. Maybe he'd get a chance to make a break.

"I'll dig," he said.

"I knew you'd see it my way," Bollen said. "Now get moving."

Fargo turned and walked to the oak trees. Their branches lashed about in the wind, and Fargo wondered how long they could stand the pressure before some of them broke.

He saw that there were actually three holes under the oaks. Each man had been digging in a separate place, as if they didn't have any real idea of the supposed treasure's location. He wondered how they knew about the oak trees in the first place. Maybe Powell had gotten a look at the map before he'd tried to rape Jezebel, and they'd figured out the location from that.

Or maybe not. Maybe his first impression had been correct and Jezebel wasn't really running away from Powell. Maybe she'd shown him the map because they were lovers. There were a few other things that were bothering Fargo, too, but he had more immediate things to worry about.

Like getting killed.

"Pick a shovel," Bollen said. "Any one you like."

They all looked the same to Fargo. He picked one up and said, "Which hole do you want me to dig in?"

"Whichever one has the treasure in it," Joe said, laughing.

Bollen and Powell laughed, too. Fargo didn't. He started digging in the closest hole.

As he dug, the sky continued to darken. It was almost as if one solid black cloud covered the entire area over the Gulf, and there were bright streaks of lightning that flickered in and out of it far out over the water.

Fargo hadn't been digging long before it started to rain. It didn't rain hard, just a light drizzle that the wind drove into his face as the oak limbs thrashed above him and the three men stood by watching him with guns in their hands.

After only a few minutes, the hole Fargo was digging filled with water.

"There's no treasure here," he said. "If I dig any farther down, I'll just be digging a well."

"You never know what you might find down at the bottom of a well," Bollen said. He didn't come to look in the hole. "But maybe you're right. Try over there."

He gestured with his pistol barrel at the hole next to the one where Fargo was digging.

Fargo looked at it and jammed the shovel into the sand.

"Could I rest for a minute?" he asked. "This sand makes for some heavy work."

"To hell with that," Bollen said. "Get cracking."

Fargo pulled the shovel out of the sand and moved to the other hole. He dug out a few scoops of sand and piled them on the side, then stopped and wiped rain water from his dripping face.

"What's the matter, Fargo?" Powell said. "Not used to hard labor?"

"That's right," Fargo said, glad that his act was giving the impression he was aiming for. "I can ride all day, but digging a hole is different."

"Damn right it is," Joe said. "That's why we're not doing it."

The others joined in his laughter, and Fargo let them enjoy Joe's wit. He wanted them relaxed.

As the hole got deeper, Fargo noticed that there was no sign of water flowing into it. He wondered why that was. This hole wasn't any different from the other one as far as he could see, and he'd expected it to fill just as quickly.

He kept on digging. If he kept going at that rate, the hole would soon be so deep he'd have to get down into it to continue. He couldn't have that, not if he wanted to escape. So he tossed aside a couple of scoops of sand and said, "I think I've hit something!"

"Hot damn!" Powell said, leaning forward. "What is it?"

"This," Fargo said, and threw a shovelful of sand in his face.

Powell gagged and stumbled backward, spitting sand. He dropped his gun and clawed at his eyes.

Fargo never stopped swinging the shovel. He let its momentum carry it straight to Bollen's wrist. There was a satisfying thud as it struck, and Bollen yelled in pain. His pistol went flying.

Letting go of the shovel, Fargo made a dive for Powell's gun. He got his hand on it just as a bullet spatted into the sand. Grit flew up into Fargo's face, but Fargo didn't let it bother him. He snatched up the pistol and shot Joe twice. The first bullet hit him in the arm, but the second took him squarely in the middle of his chest.

Joe remained standing for just a second, looking at Fargo in surprise. Then he stepped forward and almost fell into the hole that Fargo had been digging.

Fargo rolled him over and pulled his Colt from the fallen man's belt. He felt a lot better holding two guns in his hands than he had when he'd been holding only a shovel. He looked around for Bollen and Powell.

Powell was gone, but Bollen was there—and he'd found his pistol. He got off a quick shot at Fargo before slipping behind the twisted oaks.

Another shot came from the top of one of the sand dunes,

where Powell lay prone. Fargo could see the top of his head sticking up from the vines.

The only available cover for Fargo was the holes he'd been digging, and he didn't want to dive into one of them. He looked around for the dun and saw it through the thin curtain of rain. It hadn't wandered far.

Powell fired again, and Fargo made a break for the horse. When he did, Bollen stepped out from behind the oaks and added his shots to Powell's.

The wet sand seemed to drag at Fargo's boots as he ran, but he got to the dun. He was reaching for the saddle horn when somebody shot it off.

The startled horse started to run. Fargo grabbed for the saddle and missed, but he got hold of the stirrup and held on. He was jerked off his feet, but he held on as the big dun dragged him along at a rapid clip. He bounced over small dunes and nearly lost his boot when his foot caught in a vine, but soon he was out of gunshot range. He let go of the stirrup, then skidded and scraped along the sand for several feet before coming to a stop. He didn't waste any time resting. He got to his feet and took off with his long, loping stride, following the horse back to the Carson ranch.

16

Fargo was quite a sight when he arrived at the Carsons' front door. He was wet, sandy, and bedraggled.

"What the hell happened to you?" Carson asked, closing the door after Fargo was inside. He had to push hard against it because of the howling wind.

"I had a little run-in with those men who ambushed us," Fargo told him.

"I hope they look as bad as you do," Carson said.

"One of them's dead."

"Serves the bastard right. Where did all this happen?"

"At those three oak trees. They were digging for the treasure."

"Goddamnit! We have to stop them!"

"I think I did," Fargo said.

At that moment Jezebel walked into the room, and Fargo had to explain again what had happened.

"We can't let them have the treasure," she said. "We have to go after it ourselves."

"I don't think they stayed around," Fargo told her. "Not in this weather."

In fact, the weather was so bad that Fargo hadn't been sure he'd get back to the ranch house. The wind was blowing harder than he'd ever seen it blow, and the rain was coming down still harder. The drops were huge, and they stung like bees when they hit his sand-scraped face.

"Weather?" Carson said. "This ain't weather. Just a little late-summer blow. Nothing to worry about."

"I was just out there," Fargo said. "It worried me."

"It worries me, too," Jezebel said. "It could be the beginning of a hurricane."

"This?" Carson looked amazed. "You think this is a hurricane?"

"I said the *beginning* of one," Jezebel told him. "It can always get worse."

"We don't know that it will, but we sure as hell know those bastards will go back after that treasure. If you and Fargo want to say here in the house where it's nice and dry, well, you can stay. But I'm going as soon as I can get me a shovel."

"You won't need one," Fargo said. "Bollen left his there."

"He might've come back for it," Carson said. "I'm going down to the barn and get Ben. He ain't scared of a little wind and rain."

Jezebel looked helplessly at Fargo.

"Can't you talk some sense into him?" she asked.

Fargo shook his head. "Nope. He's your father, after all."

"You're right. And that means I have to go with him."

"I'm going, too," Fargo said.

"You don't have to."

"I know that. But I want to be there if Bollen shows up again."

"I don't need you to do my gunning for me," Carson said. "I can shoot as good as any man alive."

Fargo said he didn't doubt it. Then he added, "But this is getting personal."

"All right. Let's get ready. Jezebel, you get the shotgun. I'll go get Ben. We'll take the wagon."

"Do you have any rain slickers?" Fargo asked.

"Yeah. Jezebel will get 'em."

Carson started out of the room but turned back.

"What happened to Billy's horse?" he asked Fargo.

"I don't know. It was headed back this way."

"Maybe it's back at the barn by now."

"Maybe," Fargo said.

The wagon shook in the wind that howled in across the waves that rose and fell in the Gulf. The waves had foaming white crests and didn't resemble in any way the small swells that Fargo and Jezebel had been swimming in only a day or so before.

Fargo thought that any second the wagon would pitch over

on its side, but it didn't. The horse plodded along, making slow progress toward the oak trees.

There was no talking among the people in the wagon. The roaring of the waves, the wailing of the wind, and the rush of the rain made conversation of any kind impossible. Fargo sat with his back to the Gulf and watched the vines being stripped from the dunes and blown away into the darkness on the other side of the island. Fargo couldn't see where the vines went because even though it wasn't even late afternoon, the sky was as black as midnight. Fargo would have asked Carson what he thought about the weather now if he could have made himself heard.

Now and then lightning would flash overhead and illuminate the island in a pure white light for a second or two. Thunder would crash loudly. It was an oddly muffled sound, though, as if most of it was being swallowed by all the other noises of the false night.

Fargo didn't know what a hurricane was like, but if it was any worse than what they were experiencing now, he didn't want any part of one.

After what seemed like hours, they reached the place where Bollen and the others had been digging. There was no one there, however, unless you counted Joe, who hadn't left. He was still lying where he had fallen, right beside one of the holes, with his head hanging over the edge.

The shovels were still there as well. Bollen and Powell had left in a hurry. Maybe they thought Fargo would be back, or maybe they thought it would be crazy to stay any longer. If that was what they'd thought, Fargo had to give them credit for having more sense than Carson—or than him for that matter—he was there, after all, and he didn't have to be. It wasn't his treasure.

Jezebel was driving the wagon and she guided the horse behind a dune where there was at least a bit of shelter from the wind before pulling back on the reins and bringing it to a halt.

No one tried to talk, even in the relative shelter of the dune. They climbed down, and walked over to the holes.

Fargo pushed Joe's body a little to the side and pointed out the shovels that no one had bothered to carry away. Carson nodded. He walked back to the wagon and threw his own shovel in the wagon bed. If it made any noise when it hid the wood, Fargo didn't hear it.

The rain was falling so hard and the sky was so black that Fargo couldn't see very far in any direction. He could see the waves of the Gulf at the edge of where the beach had been, but the water was almost up to the holes. In another couple of hours, it would cover them, Fargo thought, if it kept on going at the same rate.

Fargo's hat was tied firmly under his chin, and water sluiced off the brim as he looked down at the holes. He wondered how long it would take Carson to give up and go home.

Carson wordlessly pointed out a hole to Ben, who started digging. It was the one that had filled with water when Fargo had been digging, and there was even more water in it now. Fargo thought it would be better just to start a new one than to continue digging in that one, but he didn't argue with Carson. He just walked over to the hole where Joe lay and left the third one for Carson.

Pushing Joe aside, Fargo saw that there was water in the hole now though none had been there earlier. Whether it was seeping in from the bottom or had collected there from the rain, he didn't know. Probably both, he thought.

They had brought a lantern with them. Jezebel had crouched under the wagon in the shelter of the dune and managed to light it. Now she stood under the oaks, holding the lantern high, but its feeble glow didn't help much. Fargo thought that the wind and the rain would douse it soon. The wind-whipped branches of the tree writhed over Jezebel's head and cast shadows that moved weirdly in the faint dim lantern light.

Digging in wet sand wasn't easy under even the best of conditions. The storm made it almost impossible. Fargo thought that he had been a fool to come along on the treasure-hunting expedition, but there were some questions that he wanted to find answers to, and he thought that he might find those answers under the oak trees. So he kept digging.

As he dug, he wondered again why Bollen had picked those three particular spots. Guesswork, Fargo thought. There was no way of knowing exactly where the treasure was supposed to be, even though there was an *X* on the map. It most likely hadn't been intended as an exact marking.

If Fargo had been burying treasure, he would have dug down near the single trunk of the entwined trees and put the chest, if there was a chest, among the roots and let them grow and wrap around it to hold it down. He thought about telling Carson his idea, but he didn't think the old man would listen. He was too wrapped up himself, wrapped up in the idea of a pirate treasure that probably didn't even exist and in the hope that the treasure was going to save his ranch.

Fargo wasn't going to be the one who told him any different.

Fifteen or twenty minutes of digging went by before Fargo was ready to give it up. He was convinced there was nothing in the hole except water, and the deeper he dug, the more water there was. He was standing in the hole, and water was up over the tops of his feet and seeping into his boots. He was about to climb out when his shovel hit something.

At first Fargo thought the resistance he felt was just his imagination. He'd told Bollen earlier that he'd hit something, but that was a lie. Now, maybe his mind was just playing tricks on him. He jammed the shovel down into the water and through the slushy sand. It met solid resistance again. There was definitely something down there. Probably only a root, Fargo told himself. The roots of the oak would be spreading out for many feet in every direction, and he'd run into one of them. He was surprised he hadn't run into one before now.

On the other hand, it might not be a root. It might be something else.

Fargo didn't say anything to anyone. He just dug a little faster, trying to clear out the area around the root. Or whatever it was.

He bent to the work, sloshing in the water and throwing it out with the sand. Jezebel noticed his increased activity and came over with the lantern. Her face was almost lost in the shadows under her hat.

Fargo looked up at her. He saw her lips moving, but the wind carried her words away before he could make them out. He shrugged and went on with what he was doing.

Before long he had cleared out an area around whatever

was at the bottom of the hole. He still couldn't see it because of the water and the darkness, so he tossed the shovel aside and put his hands into the hole.

Feeling around the object, he determined that it was probably a rectangular box of some kind. He tried to think of what kind of box, other than one filled with treasure, would be buried in the sand. He couldn't think of anything, not that made any sense. It was beginning to look as if the map was right, and as if Bollen had gotten very lucky in his choice of a place to dig.

But Bollen's luck hadn't lasted. He was gone, and the box was there for whoever found it. So it was Carson who'd really gotten lucky.

Fargo climbed out of the hole and stood beside Jezebel. He put his mouth next to her ear and said, "I think I've found something."

"The treasure?" she asked.

Fargo shrugged. He walked over to where Carson was digging and got the old man's attention. When Carson looked up, Fargo motioned for him to come along.

Carson threw his shovel down and followed Fargo. When they got to the hole, Fargo told him that there was something down there.

"Let's get Ben," Carson said.

Ben looked happy to stop digging and have a look. But there was nothing to see except dark water and sand.

"It's down there under the water," Fargo said. "We'll have to wrestle it out."

"Give him a hand, Ben," Carson said.

The two men got into the hole. It was a little crowded, especially with both of them having to bend down, but they managed to stay out of each other's way and work their hands down under the box. They tried to lift it out, but it seemed as if every time they managed to raise it a couple of inches, the sand and water sucked it back down.

"I'll have to dig it out some more," Fargo said.

Ben nodded and got out of the hole. Fargo took his shovel and started to work. He wasn't sure what was happening, but it seemed that the more he dug, the farther the box sank into the ground.

He waved Ben over and said, "I think the water's washing out the sand under the box. Bring your shovel over here."

Ben got the shovel and Fargo told him to get down in the hole.

"See if you can get the shovel under the box and hold it in place while I clear out some sand," Fargo said.

Ben put the shovel into the hole and levered it under the box. He held the box where it was, while Fargo worked at clearing sand.

"See if you can brace it," Fargo said.

Ben pushed on the shovel and wiggled it in the sand. Then he nodded.

"Let's try to get it out again," Fargo said.

They bent to it, and this time the box moved slowly out of the sand. It was quite heavy, but after a few seconds, they had muscled it onto more or less solid ground.

Carson was practically hopping with excitement. Fargo thought the old man probably didn't even know that the rain was falling in sheets or that the tree limbs above them were flailing in the wind.

There was a brilliant flash of lightning, and everyone got a good look at the box. It looked just about the way Fargo had imagined it would, a wooden rectangle about two feet long and a foot deep. The wood was waterlogged and worm-eaten, and Fargo wondered if the contents had been wrapped in something to protect them from the water and the critters.

Of course if the contents were gold, there probably wouldn't be much need for protection. Even salt and sand wouldn't do much harm to gold, and worms or crabs couldn't do it any damage at all.

The treasure of Jean Lafitte, Fargo thought, wondering what the old pirate had left for them to find.

Fargo looked around at the others. Their faces showed their anticipation. They were as eager as he was to see what the box contained.

"Let's open her up!" Carson said. "Let's have a look at the treasure."

"Sounds like a fine idea to me," Gar Bollen said.

17

Bollen and Sim Powell stepped out from behind the dunes holding their pistols and grinning with confidence.

"We figured you'd do the work for us if we waited long enough," Bollen said. "But I was beginning to wonder if we'd be able to wait long enough, what with this storm we got."

Fargo felt hollow inside. If he'd thought to search the area, maybe he'd have found Bollen. But he'd figured Bollen had left for good.

"You're not gonna get your hands on my treasure," Carson said, taking a step toward Bollen.

"Stay where you are, old man, or I'll blow your head off," Bollen said. "And I'll enjoy doing it."

Though Bollen's words were muffled by the storm, there was no doubting their sincerity. Carson froze where he was and then took a step back.

Fargo didn't bother going for his Colt. It was under his slicker, and by the time Fargo could pull the pistol, Bollen and Powell would have him filled full of holes. He needed something to distract them, but he didn't know what to do.

Jezebel did. She threw the lantern at the twisted trunk of the oak trees.

The glass smashed against the wood. There was a brief coal-oil flare-up, and then there was darkness.

Fargo threw his slicker aside and grabbed the Colt.

He was about to pull the trigger when something smashed into the side of his head.

He fell to his knees and was hit again. He fell into the hole where the treasure had been, splashing into the water, and that was the last he knew for a while.

*　　*　　*

When Fargo came to, he was suffocating. His mouth was filled with sand and there was a great weight on his chest, as if someone had put the treasure box on top of it.

He tried to move, but it was almost impossible. He wondered if he'd been tied up, though he couldn't feel any ropes.

Something covered his face. He couldn't breathe. He fought down the panic that threatened to seize him and tried to think.

Sand. He was trapped in sand. *Under* sand. Wet sand that was holding him down and pressing in on him from all sides.

That bastard Bollen had carried out his earlier promise. He'd buried Fargo alive.

Again Fargo fought against the impulse to panic. Alive. That was the important thing. He was alive. He should have been dead, though. A man buried under the sand shouldn't have lived long enough to think he was dead.

So something had kept Fargo alive. The fact that he was still alive meant that he was breathing at least a little bit.

Fargo started to dig with his hands. At the same time, he squirmed his legs. Anything to get some movement. But he couldn't use up the air too quickly. There might not be much left.

He planted his heels and thrust his body upward. He was sure he felt movement in the sand, though it was heavy upon him. They couldn't have covered him very deeply, he told himself. They would have been in too much of a hurry.

After a little more scrabbling with his hands, he realized that he wasn't alone in the hole. There was a body on top of him.

Fargo's first thought was that Bollen had killed Carson or Jezebel or both of them and tossed them in with him, but he knew that wasn't likely. He figured it was Joe.

That was probably Bollen's idea of a joke: Throw Joe into the hole with Fargo and bury them together.

But the joke had backfired. Joe's arm was over Fargo's eyes and nose, protecting them from the sand and forming a small pocket of air.

Air that wouldn't last much longer, Fargo knew. He heaved upward again, and this time he was certain that the sand had given way, though the water in the hole had mixed with the sand there and the combination was sucking him back down the way the treasure box had been sucked down.

Fargo kept working. He managed to dig one hand free, and he felt it break out of the sand. It was at that point that the air ran out. There was no more to breathe. Fargo heaved upward, wishing Joe weighed less. The sand moved, but it didn't give way. Fargo's lungs were burning and his head seemed to be swelling in its skin. He thought it would be a terrible thing to die when he was so close to getting free.

He brought his hand back into the hole. He could move both hands now, and he dug them under Joe's body and pushed. He pushed until he thought his skull would burst from the effort and his lungs would explode.

Just when he thought he could do no more, the body broke through the layer of sand that covered them.

Fargo clawed up out of the grave, spitting sand. He cleared his mouth and sat there, taking great, gasping breaths, inhaling air mixed with rain, and choking on it.

He pushed the body aside and crawled out of the grave. For a long time he lay sprawling on the sand, waiting for his breathing to return to normal.

Fargo was grateful that Bollen and Powell hadn't killed him outright. He was pleased that their sadistic little game hadn't turned out in their favor. He didn't want his life to end on some little island in the middle of a storm. He had things to do.

Fargo pushed Joe's body into the hole and stood up. His head felt about twice its normal size, and he couldn't tell if the booming sound he heard was coming from the surf or from inside his skull.

He pushed his hand under his hat and felt his head. There he found a hard knot, tender to the touch, from where he'd been hit. His hat had cushioned the blows or it would have been worse. He might not have woke up at all. But of course Bollen had wanted him to wake up. That would be part of the fun.

Fargo stumbled around looking for a horse. There wasn't one to be found, and of course the wagon was gone.

Then Fargo thought about his pistol. He reached inside the

slicker and felt the empty holster. He'd had the gun in his hand when he was hit. Either Bollen had taken it or it was in the hole with Joe.

Fargo got back into the hole, which was now Joe's grave—and Joe's alone. Feeling around in the water at the bottom, Fargo finally found the pistol under Joe's body. When he brought it out, he made sure the barrel was clear of water and sand, then put the pistol in its holster.

Once again he climbed out of the hole. His head was still pounding, but his mind was clearing. He figured he knew where he had to go. He just wasn't sure he could get there. It was going to be a long walk for any man, much less one who was supposed to be dead.

And nearly was.

The storm made any kind of traveling difficult, and Fargo didn't make much progress. His long stride normally ate up the ground, but the storm was against him. The rain and wind and rising water made walking difficult at best, and at times it was almost impossible. More than once, Fargo was forced to go some distance out of his way to avoid having to wade in water that was up to his calves.

The Trailsman was convinced that if he wasn't in the middle of a hurricane, he soon would be. He was also certain that the entire island was going to be under water before the night was over. There was no high ground to climb to for protection, so the safest place would be on the second floor of one of the built-up houses in town, and that was where Fargo was headed.

The way he saw it, Jed Gunn was behind everything that had happened. Powell and Bollen were working for him. Fargo hadn't figured out all the details yet, and he had a nagging feeling that he'd heard or been told something that should have been a clue to him. It was itching at the back of his mind, but he couldn't quite bring it to the front.

He thought he had most of it figured out, though. If he was right, Jezebel and Carson would be at Gunn's place. That is, they would if Bollen hadn't killed them yet. There wasn't much doubt that sooner or later that was what would happen.

Gunn might not want it that way, and in fact he probably

didn't. He might still be in love with Jezebel, which would explain why she and Carson had been taken instead of killed. But what Gunn wanted might not matter.

Fargo didn't believe Gunn could control Bollen. You could hire a man like Bollen and point him in the direction you wanted him to go, but after that, Bollen would do pretty much as he pleased.

In fact, he might just take the treasure for himself. If he did that, the question was whether he'd let Gunn have a look at it before he killed him and everybody else involved.

Fargo's clothes were just about soaked through even though he was still wearing the slicker. What with the wind driving the rain at a slant, the slicker wasn't doing all that much good. Fargo wiped water out of his eyes and kept walking.

Finally, after a very long time, he came to the outskirts of town. He could see the dark outlines of the houses as he passed them, but the town was dark. There were no gaslights to illumine the night. Fargo thought the storm was to blame for that.

There were probably people awake inside the houses, waiting out the storm, but the only lights that showed were faint lines of lamplight at the edges of the boards that covered the windows. There was no one outside except Fargo. Water was running in the streets, and the wind seemed about to tear his slicker off and carry it away.

After a while Fargo located the street where the Gunns' house was. It sat up higher than many of the others, and Fargo thought that it stood as good a chance as any structure on the island of remaining dry.

Even if Fargo was all wrong, even if Bollen wasn't there, the house would be a good place to wait for the storm to subside. But Fargo didn't think he was wrong.

Before he got to the end of the block, he could see a light shining around the edges of the boards on one of the first floor windows.

He sloshed down the street and pushed through the gate, then went up the walk and onto the porch. He couldn't very well go to the door and knock, but he was glad for the shelter of the porch roof and for the walls of the house. For the first time in quite a while, he was protected from the wind and water, and he took advantage of the situation to sit down and rest with his back against the wall. He didn't think anyone was going to come out there looking for him.

Fargo sat there for several minutes with water running off him and soaking into the already wet boards of the porch. He couldn't hear anything from inside the house, but that was no surprise. The wind was moaning around the corners and the trees and bushes were thrashing in the yard. Fargo could even hear the booming of the surf, though the beach wasn't really very near. He got up and moved to the window where he'd seen the light.

Between two of the boards there was a crack big enough to see through, and Fargo bent down and peered into the house.

The big front parlor was a mess, with pools of water on the hardwood floor. Sand and grit were everywhere. The treasure box was in the middle of the room. The lid had been pried off, and it lay to one side of the box as if carelessly tossed there. The box itself, as far as Fargo could tell, was empty. He knew it hadn't been that way when it came out of the hole. It had been too heavy.

Jezebel and Carson were there, too, tied to two straight-backed chairs. They were wet and bedraggled. Jezebel's hat was missing, and her hair had come undone. It hung in thick damp strands about her face.

Carson looked old and tired and beaten. He had come within inches of having his treasure, and it had been wrested from him. His head was down, his bearded chin resting on his chest.

There was no one else in the room. Fargo figured that Gunn and Bollen had removed the treasure to somewhere safer, somewhere out of sight. They were probably dividing it now, if Bollen hadn't killed the others and taken it all for himself.

Getting into the house wasn't going to be easy, Fargo thought. He couldn't just pull the boards off the window. Someone was sure to hear him.

Fargo wondered if anyone was guarding the other entrances to the house. Probably not, he thought. They didn't have any reason to expect company. He was sure they thought the crabs were eating him by this time, the way they were eating Joe and Willie.

How many men were in the house? Assuming that everyone involved was inside, there were at least four: Powell, Bollen, Gunn, and Ben.

It had taken Fargo a while to figure out about Ben, but it seemed obvious now. According to Flora, there had been a falling out between Ben and his brother about Jezebel, who hadn't responded to them. How better to get back at the Carsons than by stealing their treasure? Both Ben and Billy would have known about the treasure, and it had to be one of them who had told Jed Gunn.

Whichever one it had been, Fargo thought that Ben had betrayed both his brother and the Carsons in the end. Ben and Billy had most likely been meeting with Bollen at the barn on the previous day and set up the ambush. Billy had been killed immediately, and with him out of the way, Ben would get a greater share of the treasure. He might even think he'd have a chance with Jezebel.

Ben would also have told Bollen where to dig. By sinking three holes, Bollen had gotten lucky, though he didn't know it at the time. He knew it now, though, and he had the treasure.

The matter of the poisoned cattle bothered Fargo, too. Who had been doing the poisoning? Ben and Billy, of course. They could have done it easily and without having to worry about being caught. They were supposed to be the ones guarding the cattle.

Fargo wasn't sure whether poison had actually been used. There were other ways of killing cattle and controlling the number that died. Gunn wouldn't want a ranch with no cattle on it, so the fewer that died, the better, from his point of view.

Then there was the matter of the fight at the Gunns' house. Ben hadn't taken any part in it. He'd had a ready answer to explain why, even before anyone questioned him about it, but thinking back, that just fueled Fargo's suspicions.

And of course someone had told Powell and Bollen Fargo's name. Ben would be the one who'd done that as well.

The clincher was that Ben was the only person who could have hit Fargo in the back of the head at the oak trees. Bollen and Powell had been standing in front of him, and Jezebel and Carson had been to his side. Ben was the only one left to hit him. Fargo owed him for that, if for nothing else. And Fargo was a man who liked to pay his debts.

But first he had to get into the house. He knew about the back entrance, but it was possible that everyone was in the kitchen counting the treasure. It wouldn't be a good idea to try that way, not if it meant walking in on the whole lot of them. They would be surprised, and that was in Fargo's favor, but they had the numbers on their side.

He thought about climbing to the second floor, but the windows up there were boarded up just like the ones on the first floor and would present the same problems.

What problems? It occurred to Fargo that his fear of being heard was groundless. With the noise of the storm, no one was going to hear a few boards being peeled off the window frames, not if he did it carefully. And the best place to enter would be the room where Jezebel and Carson were tied up. There was no guard because no one expected trouble from an old man and a woman who were safely tied up.

And no one expected trouble from Fargo. He was supposed to be a dead man, lying in a hole near the beach with the back of his head caved in.

He tested one of the boards. It had been nailed in tightly, but by putting his fingers into the crack he had looked through, he was able to get considerable leverage. He put his left foot against the wall and pushed hard while pulling back with both hands.

The nails that held the board began to ease out of the wall. There was a slight screeching noise, but Fargo could hardly hear it himself. He was certain no one in the house could hear, though Jezebel and Carson would see what was happening. Fargo hoped they'd keep quiet.

When he had the board completely removed, he laid it on the porch and looked into the room. Jezebel was staring back at him, her eyes wide with disbelief and surprise. Fargo didn't blame her. She had probably thought that she'd never see him again, and he probably looked like some kind of ghost, blown in on the wind of the storm.

Carson wasn't looking. His head was still down on his chest. Fargo wondered if the old man was still alive. The storm and the excitement might have been too much for him.

Fargo put a finger to his lips to signal Jezebel to be quiet. She nodded and then inclined her head to the left, which Fargo took to mean that Bollen and the others were somewhere nearby. He indicated that he understood and took another board off the window.

Soon he had removed enough boards to give him access to the room. He hoped the window wasn't locked. He gave it a try, and it moved slowly upward. He pushed it about halfway up, bent over, and stepped over the sill and into the room.

18

Fargo heard voices in another room, people talking, arguing over something. The voices were muffled by the wash of the rain over the house, and Fargo couldn't really tell what they were saying. He didn't pay much attention to them, and he didn't think anyone would be paying attention to a few noises from the room where he was, either.

He untied Jezebel, who whispered, "Is it really you?"

"It's me, all right," Fargo told her. "What's left of me."

"I thought you were dead for sure."

"I'm harder to kill than some people think," Fargo said. He looked at Carson.

"He's all right," Jezebel whispered. "I think he's asleep."

Fargo must have looked surprised because Jezebel continued, "He can sleep anywhere, any time. He told me not to worry, that you'd be here to help us. I didn't believe him. They buried you alive!"

"That was their mistake," Fargo said.

Fargo shook Carson's shoulder gently, and the old man's head came up. His eyes fastened on Fargo's, and his mouth smiled beneath the beard. He didn't say a word.

The ropes fell to the floor when Fargo undid the knots, and Carson stood up. Fargo pointed toward the window. Carson nodded, and the three of them left the room the way Fargo had entered.

When they were safely on the porch, Fargo tried to replace the boards, but it proved to be impossible. He'd bent the nails, and they wouldn't go back smoothly into their holes.

Carson tugged at his sleeve.

"Leave 'em be," he said. "Let's move on around to the other side."

The porch extended around three sides of the house, and Carson led Fargo and Jezebel around the corner. The wind and rain were much stronger there, and Fargo said, "We need to get shelter from the hurricane."

Carson laughed. "Son, this ain't a hurricane. It's just a little rainstorm." He sobered. "But the real thing's coming along any minute now. I can smell it."

Fargo wondered how that was possible. If he could smell anything at all it was the rain that filled the air, soaked his clothes, and beat at the roof of the porch.

"We have to get my treasure back before it hits," Carson said.

"There really was treasure in that box?" Fargo said.

"Yep. Gold bullion, shining like a star, like it came from the hold of Jean Lafitte's ship just yesterday. I don't guess we ever really believed it would be there. We just hoped it would. But there it was, and I'll be as rich as any man in Galveston when I get my hands on it."

Getting their hands on it wasn't going to be easy, Fargo thought. He said, "How many men are in the house?"

"Three," Jezebel said. "Or that's how many we know about. Gar Bollen, Sim Powell, and Ben."

"That son of a bitch," Carson said. "I treated him and his brother right, and he turned on me. 'Course Jezebel kinda hurt his feelings, and Billy's too, but there's no excuse for what he did." Carson shook his head. "Threw in with the men that killed his brother. You can't get much lower than that."

Fargo didn't mention his idea that Ben had been in on other things, too, like the cattle poisoning. He said, "What about Jed Gunn?"

"Now that's the curious thing," Carson said. "You'd think he'd be there to divide up the treasure, but we didn't see hide nor hair of him."

"Bollen may have killed him," Fargo said.

"Don't know about that. All I know is, they're in the kitchen now, arguing over something. I don't know who's in there with 'em. Maybe Jed showed up late. I don't imagine he wanted me and Jezebel to see him. He was kinda sweet on Jezebel at one time, which is probably why he hasn't had us killed yet. But he was getting to it. Nothing else he could do, not if he aimed to keep that treasure."

"How did you know I was coming?" Fargo asked.

"Didn't," Carson said. "Just figured you for having a hard head. And I knew they shoulda killed you instead of getting fancy. They thought it was a real big joke to put you under that sand while you were still breathing. They shoulda known that if they wanted to get rid of a man like you, they'd have to put a bullet in his head."

"I'm glad they didn't," Fargo said.

"So am I," Jezebel told him.

Carson ignored them both. He said, "Besides, if you was alive, I knew when you worked out who it was that hit you, you'd want to do something about it even if you didn't want to help me and Jezebel. So the question is, what're we gonna do, now that you're here?"

"We're going to get that treasure," Fargo said.

"Hell, I know that. But how do we go about it?"

"That's the part I haven't quite worked out yet."

"I got an idea," Carson said.

"Let's hear it," Fargo said.

They were back inside the room, with Carson and Jezebel sitting in the chairs, the ropes arranged around them so that they appeared to be tied.

Fargo stood to one side of the door leading out of the room into the hallway, his gun in one hand and a small end table in the other.

When Carson nodded, Fargo began to bang against the wall with the table. He hit it so hard the second time that the table splintered into pieces, leaving Fargo holding only the leg. He was sure they heard that in the other room, no matter how loudly the storm was raging outside.

All conversation in the other room ceased. There was nothing to hear other than the wind and the rain.

Fargo waited. After a short time, the door swung open. Fargo was concealed behind it when Ben stepped into the room, holding his pistol and looking around.

"What the hell's going on?" he said.

"Somebody's in the house," Carson said. "Tore the boards right off the window. Then he ran by us and went on upstairs."

"You sure about that?"

"If you don't believe me, have a look at the window," Carson said.

Ben took another step into the room, and the door swung closed behind him.

Fargo swung the table leg with all his might, slamming it into the back of Ben's head. The leg was as flimsy as the table had been, and it broke in half in Fargo's hand.

Ben took a couple of stagger-steps, trying to turn around to see what had hit him, but he didn't get far. Jezebel and Carson came off the chairs. Jezebel grabbed Ben's gun hand and twisted. Carson hit him in the face. When Ben started to crumple, Carson hit him again.

Ben dropped to the floor, leaving Jezebel with his pistol. She leveled it at the door, which flew open in a gust of wind from the outside.

But there was no one to be seen behind it. Powell and Bollen had gone.

"Damn!" Carson said.

He rushed down the hall to the kitchen.

"It's all right!" he called. "They left the gold!"

Fargo bent down to check on Ben, whose eyes were rolled up in his head. He didn't seem likely to give any trouble for a while, but Fargo used the ropes to tie him, just in case.

When he was finished, Fargo stood up and said, "Is the gold all there?"

"Far as I can tell," Carson yelled. "Ten solid gold bars. They were too heavy for anybody to carry off."

Jezebel and Fargo joined him in the kitchen. Carson was closing the door, which had been left open when the men left the room.

There on the table were the gold bars. Fargo reached out a hand and touched one. It was smooth and hard and shiny in the lamplight.

"They wouldn't have gone far," he said. "Not if they had to leave all this behind."

"They heard what was going on and knew it was all over," Carson said. "They ran like rats."

"Maybe," Fargo said, not believing it.

Gar Bollen wasn't the kind of man to leave gold behind, not unless he had a plan to get it back.

While Fargo was wondering what the plan was, the door opened. Wind howled, and rain blew into the room. Both Jezebel and Fargo were ready to shoot whoever stepped inside until they saw who it was.

"Don't shoot," Amanda Gunn said. "It's only me."

She shoved the door shut behind her. She was wearing riding clothes, and the rain had plastered them to her so that every curve of her body was revealed. Fargo remembered them well enough.

"What are you doing here?" Jezebel asked.

Amanda ignored her. She was looking at Fargo.

"They said you were dead," she told him.

"They were about half right," Fargo said. "Where are they?"

"And where's that son-of-a-bitch brother of yours?" Carson asked.

"Isaiah has him," Amanda said. "Him and those two men he hired. They're all in his quarters. You have to help me, or he'll kill them."

"Who's Isaiah?" Carson asked.

"He's a slave. He's worked for our family since Jed and I were children. I never thought he'd turn on us. He says he's going to kill Jed if we don't give him the gold."

Her eyes went to the bullion on the table.

"I don't get it," Carson said. "What the hell does a slave have to do with all this? And why does he have your brother?"

"I guess you know Jed planned to get this gold from you," Amanda said.

"I knew it, all right. Ben told him about it to get back at my daughter."

Amanda paused for a contemptuous glance at Jezebel, who smiled sweetly at her.

"Jed thought it would be a good idea to get the money from you. When he heard about some men who were nosing around the island, talking about treasure, he hired them to get it for him, instead. He promised them a share."

"I don't see what this has to do with Isaiah," Fargo said.

"Jed hasn't treated Isaiah well, not the way our parents did. He beats him, and he beats his wife, too. Isaiah could take a beating of his own, but he can't stand to see it happen to Lucinda. He's been talking to some other slaves, and he got the idea of a rebellion. There are a lot of slaves, and they could take over Galveston. All they would need is a little organization and some money. As soon as he heard about the treasure, he knew how to get the money. And when they found it tonight, he kidnapped me."

"You don't look kidnapped to me," Carson said. "You just look wet."

Amanda pushed her hair, made darker red by the rain, away from her face.

"He held me to get Jed," she said. "But that didn't get him the gold. Something scared the men who had it, and they ran out into the storm. Now Isaiah has them all."

"We scared them," Fargo said, thinking that now he knew why Bollen and Powell had run. They would have had no idea who was in the front room. It could have been a dozen slaves for all they knew. But they'd run the wrong way, and now Isaiah had them.

"I guess you did scare them," Amanda said. "Anyway, Isaiah let me come here to tell you that unless you give him the gold, he's going to kill Jed and those two men."

"Let him kill the sons of bitches," Carson said. "I don't give a damn what happens to them, as long as I have my treasure. Come on, Fargo. Let's get it out of here and down to my ranch where it belongs."

As soon as Carson had finished speaking, Amanda started snuffling, and within seconds she was weeping uncontrollably. Her face was red, and she breathed in great gulps of air between sobs.

Even Jezebel seemed to feel sorry for her. She went over to Amanda and put her arm around the redhead's shaking shoulders.

"Don't cry," Jezebel said. "We'll get Jed back for you."

"Oh, thank you. I knew I could count on you. Jed always liked you."

"We're not doing it because of that."

"But you'll do it?"

Jezebel looked at Fargo and Carson. Both men were shaking their heads. Jezebel narrowed her eyes at them.

"Of course we will," she said. "Isn't that right, Fargo?"

Fargo didn't think it was right, and he was sure Carson didn't think so, either.

For his part, Fargo didn't trust Amanda. She looked and sounded quite convincing, and she had told Fargo she wasn't the one he'd seen riding with Gar Bollen, but he never believed her. He wasn't sure the tears she was crying now were entirely persuasive, either.

But no matter how Fargo felt, Jezebel was persuaded. Her look had changed to a glare.

Well, Fargo thought, Amanda had told him how she and Jed stuck up for each other, and maybe that's what she was doing now, sticking up for her brother. If she wasn't, they'd find out.

"All right," he said. "We'll see what we can do."

"The hell we will," Carson said. "The son of a bitch tried to take my ranch. We're getting out of here with the gold."

"He never cared about your ranch," Amanda said. "You think he'd take it just because your daughter slighted him? He's not that kind of man."

"The hell he's not," Carson said.

"It doesn't matter what kind of man he is," Jezebel said. "We can't let him die because of us."

"Yes, we can," Carson told her.

Jezebel left Amanda's side and walked over to her father. She looked him straight in the eye.

"Oh, no we can't," she said.

Carson held her gaze for a second or two, but then he dropped his eyes.

"Ah, hell," he said.

Fargo tried not to laugh. He said, "There's a hurricane blowing out there."

"That's still not a hurricane," Carson reminded him. "But one's coming."

"Then we'd better hurry," Amanda said. "How can we carry the gold?"

"We'll have to leave it here," Fargo said. "If they want it so much, let them come and get it."

Amanda looked doubtful, but she said, "Very well. I suppose they'll know we didn't carry it away and bury it."

Fargo didn't like to think about burying anything. It was an uncomfortable reminder of where he'd been not so very long ago. He was also still wondering what was really going to happen when they got to Isaiah's living quarters.

He supposed there was one way to find out. He pushed open the kitchen door.

It had stopped raining, and the wind seemed to have dropped. The silence was almost eerie. Fargo turned to Carson.

"Looks like the storm's over," he said.

"Nope," Carson said. "It's just starting."

Fargo started to reply, but before the words were out of his mouth, there was a roaring like the sound of a runaway train. And then the wind hit.

The wind tore the door from Fargo's hands and slammed it back against the wall. It rushed through the house, rattling the pots and pans in the kitchen and shaking the furniture.

The rain followed, coming in a torrent that inundated Fargo and washed across the floor.

"We have to go for Jed!" Amanda yelled. "Before it's too late."

Fargo thought it was already too late. He wasn't sure they could even stand up outside the house, much less get to the smaller building where Isaiah and his wife lived.

As if to prove him wrong, Amanda walked across the room and out the door. She was bent against the force of the wind, but she was able to stand. Fargo watched her make her way down the steps.

"Well?" Jezebel shouted. "What are you waiting for?"

Fargo wanted to say he was waiting for the storm to end, but he didn't think that would be a good idea. So he shrugged and followed Amanda.

The wind nearly tore his clothes off, and the raindrops slapped into him like shotgun pellets. He heard something that sounded like rifle shots and peered through the darkness at a huge tree that had cracked in the middle as it was twisted in the hurricane's grip. Pieces of someone's roof whipped by Fargo's head and slammed into the wall of the Gunns' house.

Somehow Fargo managed to keep walking, though it seemed at every step he might be toppled over and rolled across the lawn like a child's corncob doll. He didn't look back to see if Jezebel and Carson were behind him. He hoped, however, that they'd had enough sense to stay inside the house.

He reached Isaiah's house almost as soon as Amanda did, and she began pounding on the door.

For a moment Fargo didn't think anyone was going to open it, but eventually it swung back slightly, revealing a thin line of light.

When whoever was inside saw that Amanda was standing there, the door opened farther, and Amanda entered. Fargo looked back then and he saw that Carson and Jezebel were only a step or so behind. Assured that they were all right, he followed Amanda into the house.

Once inside, he wiped water from his face and tried to see who was in the room.

Bollen was there—and Powell. Both held pistols and wore big grins. They didn't look anything like prisoners. Jed Gunn was there, too, tied to a chair. His mouth was covered with a cloth gag that was tied in a hard knot in the back of his head. He was a prisoner, all right.

"Never thought I'd see you again, Fargo," Bollen said. His wet hat was pushed up on his head, and his mad eyes reflected red in the lamplight. "You're sure as hell beginning to irritate me. I should've known better than to try to get fancy with you. I should have plugged you when I had the chance. In fact, I guess I should just shoot you right now and get it over with."

"Not yet," said someone from a darkened corner of the room.

Fargo recognized the voice. Isaiah walked into the circle of lamplight. He too held a pistol, and he looked nothing at all like the man Fargo had see the night before or earlier that day. He looked younger, for one thing, and about a hundred times more dangerous for another. He stood tall and straight, and he wasn't grinning like Bollen and Powell. He was as solemn as a preacher at a funeral.

"Not ever," Carson said at Fargo's back. "You want the goddman gold? Well, you can have it. It's in the kitchen over at the house. Give us Jed, and go get it."

"I'm afraid that's not exactly the plan," Isaiah said. "Is it, Amanda?"

Amanda walked over and stood beside him.

"No," she said. "That's not the plan at all."

19

"I wish someone would tell me what the hell is going on around here," Carson said.

Fargo thought he knew the answer. It had finally come to him. Too late, but the thing that had been nagging at him had managed to make it from the back of his mind to the front. Earlier that day when he'd talked to Amanda, he'd said someone had been killing Carson's cattle, and Amanda had said she didn't know anything about poisoning. Not killing. Poisoning. How had she known that?

Carson hadn't mentioned poison when they'd interrupted Amanda's party. Nor had anyone else. But Amanda had known. Ben had told her of course, which wasn't surprising. It had been Amanda all along, not Jed, who was obviously not involved at all except as Amanda's dupe. Which explained why Amanda was standing there by Isaiah and why no one was making a move to set Jed free.

So Jed had been telling the truth all along. For that matter, so had Amanda, at least part of the time. Jed didn't know a thing about his sister riding with Bollen because he didn't know about the poisoning or anything else that was going on. Amanda had kept him in the dark.

Fargo wondered what the real story was.

Why was Jed tied up?

What was Isaiah's part in the plan?

And why did Amanda want to kill the cattle and take the ranch?

Fargo couldn't quite figure it all out. So he decided to ask.

"Why?" he said.

No one spoke for a while. Outside the small house the wind lashed the trees and ripped roofs off houses. It tore away the boards that had been nailed over windows and threw limbs to smash the glass. It heaved waves from the depths of the Gulf and sent them rushing across the island. Isaiah's house wasn't raised like the Gunns', and water had begun to come in under the walls and spread across the floor.

"Why what?" Carson asked after a few seconds. "Will somebody tell me what in the name of God is happening here?"

"I think Amanda is the one who's been after the ranch and the treasure," Jezebel said. "I don't think Jed knew anything about what was going on."

"What?" Carson said. "Amanda? Why?"

"That's what Fargo wants to know," Jezebel said. "That's what everyone wants to know. Go ahead and tell us, Amanda."

"You should know, you big cow," Amanda said, venom dripping from every word. "My brother cared more about you than he did about me, and you wouldn't even look at him. You made him weak."

"What she means is, you took his attention away from her," Fargo said to Jezebel. He was beginning to understand. "She's jealous. That's all it is. This whole thing was caused by jealousy. She wants to ruin you and your father to prove to Jed that she's better than you."

"You shut up!" Amanda snapped. "I took you away from the cow."

"You didn't take me away from anyone," Fargo said.

Amanda laughed. "I'm sure you were thinking of her this afternoon, weren't you. I took you, all right, and I would have gotten Jed back, too."

"The same way?" Fargo asked.

"Shut up!" Amanda yelled. "Shut up, or I'll let Gar kill you right now."

"He can try," Fargo said. "It didn't work out so well the first time, though."

"I think we should put a stop to all this, Miss Amanda," Isaiah said, plainly uncomfortable with the way the discussion was going. "I don't like mistreating Mr. Jed like we are, and I don't see the need for any killing."

"Well," Bollen said, "that's the difference between you and me."

He pulled the trigger of his pistol and flame jumped from the barrel. Even with the noise of the storm outside, the sound of the shot was thunderous in the small room.

The only person who didn't hear it was Isaiah, who stumbled backward into the dark corner where he'd been hidden at first. This time there was a bullet hole in the middle of his face. He stood against the wall for a couple of seconds and then slid down it and into the water that was now a half inch or more deep on the floor.

Above the gag, Jed's eyes bugged in his frightened face and Amanda turned white with rage.

"You bastard!" she screamed at Bollen. "You dirty bastard!"

"That's enough of that shit," Bollen said.

He stepped over to Amanda and slapped the side of her face, hard. Her head snapped to the side, and she fell to the floor with a splash. Whether she had fainted or been hit too hard, Fargo couldn't tell.

Powell watched it all with a grin, his pistol aimed at Fargo steady as a stone.

"Now, then," Bollen said, hitching at his pants with one hand. "Sim and I are tired of messing around. We're not much at being told what to do, so we're taking charge of things from now on in."

"You'd better watch him, Sim," Fargo said. "He'll kill you next."

Bollen laughed. "Hell, Fargo, I can't do that. I need him to help me carry the gold."

Sim tried to laugh, too, but it came out as more of a squeak. To Fargo, Sim looked a little scared of Bollen. Fargo didn't blame him.

"You won't get far in this storm," Fargo said. He looked at Carson. "This *is* a storm, isn't it?"

"You could call it one, I guess," Carson said. "Not a big one, though."

"Big enough," Fargo said.

"Me and Sim aren't worried about any storm," Bollen said. "The only question is whether we kill you now or wait till later."

"Better do it now," Sim said. "Fargo don't seem to go down easy."

"Fine by me," Bollen said. "You can do him, Sim, seeing as how he killed your pard."

Powell thumbed back the hammer of his pistol.

A door opened from a back room, and Powell turned, firing as he did. Wood chunks jumped off the door, and Fargo jumped for Bollen, hoping someone else would take Powell.

Bollen, who had turned toward the door, spun around and clubbed Fargo with his pistol. Fargo saw the blow coming and managed to turn aside quickly enough to take the brunt on his shoulder, but it was the shoulder that had been wounded by Lute Hawkins only a week earlier. Pain shot from the shoulder all the way down to Fargo's toes, and it froze him just long enough for Bollen to hit him again, this time on the side of the head.

Bright lights sparked in Fargo's eyes. There was a shot, but Fargo didn't know who fired it or if anyone was hit. He tried to stand up, but his knees were too wobbly. There was another shot, and then he fell into blackness.

"Is he all right?" Jezebel asked.

Her voice seemed to come from somewhere very far away. Fargo opened his eyes and looked up into Carson's face.

"He's alive," Carson said. "I don't know about all right."

Fargo said, "I'm fine."

Or that's what he tried to say. It came out sounding more like "Ahm fi—." Getting hit on the head twice in one night didn't agree with him.

He closed his eyes and lay back on the floor. He thought he heard someone sobbing, but he didn't know for sure.

The next time Fargo came to, he was still on the floor. He had no idea how long he'd been out, but he could no longer hear the roaring of the storm.

He sat up and looked around. Jed Gunn was still sitting in the chair, but he was untied. Jezebel and Carson were standing beside him, talking in low tones. The door to the back room was open, and someone was moving around in there. He didn't see Amanda, Powell, or Bollen. Isaiah's body was gone, too.

"He's awake," Jed Gunn said.

"'Bout time," Carson said. "Maybe your head ain't as hard as I thought it was."

"I'm beginning to wonder about it, myself," Fargo said. "What happened?"

"Lucinda—that's Isaiah's wife—came in with a rifle and started shooting. Didn't do Isaiah much good, though. She's not much of a shot. Shot up the walls and the ceiling, so she didn't hurt anybody."

"Isaiah always doted on Amanda," Jed said, shaking his head. "But he was an honest man. I can't believe she got him involved in this and got him killed. She even turned him against *me* somehow."

"She was a good liar," Fargo said. "There's no telling what she might've said to him . . . or done for him. Where is he now?"

"Lucinda's with him in the back room," Jezebel said. "Amanda came to in time to make a choice about which side she wanted to be on. Bollen and Powell ran out, and she ran with them."

The three of them might have managed to carry most of the gold, Fargo thought, now that the storm was over.

"Did anybody try to stop them?" he asked.

"They had more guns than we did," Carson said. "Besides, they won't get far."

"Why not?"

"Because they think the storm's over, and it ain't. What we're in now is called the eye. That's a big calm space in the middle of a hurricane. Before long, the wind will be back, and the water will rise some more. They won't be able to get off the island, with the gold or without it."

"So all we have to do is find them," Fargo said.

"That's all," Carson said. "How's that head of yours? You ready to get started?"

Fargo's head hurt like hell.

"Later," he said.

Lucinda had Isaiah laid out on the bed. There were candles burning in the room, and the light made flickering shadows on the wall. The storm was roaring again, and the water on the floor was now a couple of inches deep.

"Isaiah raise that little girl like she was his own," Lucinda said, looking at the body of her husband. "He love her like his own child."

"Our parents died when she was small," Jed explained to Fargo. "I was old enough to take over the business, but not old enough to raise a sister, at least I didn't think I was."

"She love you, though," Lucinda said. "Maybe she love you too much."

"It wasn't a healthy attachment," Jed admitted. "And she couldn't seem to keep her hands off the men."

Fargo thought of Ben, who he assumed was still in the other house. That is, he was unless the others had freed him. Fargo couldn't see Bollen doing that under ordinary circumstances, but he might have wanted Ben's help in carrying the gold.

"Is that true, Fargo?" Jezebel asked. "That she couldn't keep her hands off the men?"

Fargo didn't feel like talking about that, but he said, "I don't know, but she used men to get what she wanted. She used Ben to poison the cattle and to find out about the map. I think she used Isaiah to find Bollen and Powell. Those two are dangerous, but they might not come out of this as well as they think if they don't keep an eye on her."

"We should check on Ben," Jezebel said. "They might have killed him."

"Don't give a damn if they did," Carson said.

"They might have left some of the gold," Fargo said. "We'll see as soon as the storm dies down."

"Won't be long," Carson said. "Good thing it wasn't a bad one. Coulda washed everything on this island away."

"There aren't any storms that bad," Jezebel said.

"Shows what you know," Carson said. "Let's just hope you never find out any different."

"Where do you think they might go with the gold?" Fargo asked.

"Don't have any idea. They brought us here in our wagon, so maybe they loaded it up and took off."

"For where? Jed?"

Jed shook his head. He didn't know, either.

"As soon as that wind drops," Fargo said, "we'll check the house."

"What if they're still there?" Carson asked.

"I hope they are," Fargo said.

20

Ben was gone.

So was the gold.

"Dammit all to hell," Carson said. "How are we gonna find 'em? This whole island will be in an uproar when the sun comes up, and that won't be more than an hour."

"What about it, Jed?" Fargo said. "You know Amanda better than anybody. Where would they go?"

"We don't know that Amanda's in control of things," Jed said in a worried voice. "That Bollen is a crazy man. You saw how he shot Isaiah."

"He won't kill Amanda," Jezebel said. "I'm sure she has something he wants."

"There's no call for that kind of talk," Jed said. "We don't know that Amanda—"

"The hell we don't," Carson said. "But it don't matter anyhow. Just try to think where they might've gone."

Jed put one of the kitchen chairs upright and sat down.

"They have to get off the island," he said. "If the railroad's still operating, which I doubt, they could go that way."

"What about a boat?" Carson said. "Did Amanda know anybody with a boat?"

"All the boats will be wrecked," Jed said. "The storm will have taken care of that."

"She coulda had one hid out," Carson said.

"Where? There's nowhere on this island that wasn't touched by the storm."

"So it's the railroad," Fargo said. "We'll go to the depot as soon as it's light."

"I just don't believe they'd go that way," Jezebel said. "They'd know they'd never get away, not after the storm."

"They weren't expecting a hurricane," Carson pointed out. "Kinda messed up their plans."

"How could they get away even if there hadn't been a storm?" Jed asked. "The depot is the first place anybody would look."

"They probably didn't intend to leave anybody alive," Fargo said.

"Woulda killed us earlier if it wasn't for Ben," Carson said. "They were talking about it. Ben's a son of a bitch, but he did talk 'em out of that. I gotta give him credit where it's due."

"It's a good thing Lucinda came out with that rifle," Fargo said. "Or we'd all be dead now."

Carson scratched his beard. "Wish she'd hit one of the bastards. Woulda saved us a lot of trouble. Anyway, what're we gonna do?"

"Wait," Fargo said.

"What the hell for?"

"So we can see," Fargo said. "The storm might be over, but it's still darker than the inside of a buffalo's gut. They won't get far."

"Amanda knows the island well," Jed said. "Even in the dark."

"We need some rest," Fargo said. "We'll wait. I could stand to lie down for a while."

"The bedrooms are upstairs," said Jed.

Jezebel looked at Fargo with suspicion, as if wondering if he'd been in the bedrooms before. Fargo wasn't admitting anything.

"Show us where," he said.

Fargo lay on the soft bed and tried to relax. He'd taken off his wet clothes and dried himself as best he could, but although he closed his eyes and lay quietly, he couldn't seem to drift off. Maybe it was because of the pounding in his head, or maybe it was because he was worried about what might happen to Amanda, not that he had any reason to care. Their brief fling had been fun, but it had meant little to either one of them aside from the momentary pleasure it had provided them. Amanda had been trying to use him the same way she'd used others. Fargo was glad she'd been only partially successful.

134

The darkness inside the room and outside the window was still nearly complete, though Fargo expected the gray of dawn in a short time. He still didn't know what he was going to do when dawn came, however.

He was thinking about that when the door to the room opened and someone came in.

Fargo's eyes were adjusted to the darkness well enough for him to distinguish that it was Jezebel. She stood silently for a moment and then said, "Did you and Amanda do it in here?"

"Do what?" Fargo asked.

"You know what."

"It didn't mean anything," Fargo said. "I get the feeling that she'd rather have had Jed."

"That's an awful thing to say. You shouldn't talk like that."

Fargo could see that Jezebel was wrapped in a sheet or robe. He wondered what was under it.

"There's something wrong with her," Fargo said. "She's twisted on the inside."

"And according to her I'm the one to blame."

"I wouldn't let that worry me if I were you. She just happened to pick you because of Jed."

"She called me a cow."

"She probably wishes she was bigger," Fargo said. "Some people are like that. They have to make fun when they can't think of anything else to do."

"Do you think I'm a cow?"

"Not hardly," Fargo said.

"Prove it," Jezebel said, throwing aside her wrap and walking over to the bed.

"What will your father and Jed think?"

"They're asleep."

"We might wake them."

"We can try," Jezebel said, sliding onto the bed beside Fargo and taking his shaft in her hand.

It was already hard, which surprised Fargo a little. You'd think that with the time he'd spent getting hit on the head, buried alive, and trudging through a hurricane, he'd be a tad too tired to respond. But maybe a man didn't ever get too tired or beat up to enjoy certain things.

Jezebel must have been tired, too, but Fargo wouldn't have

guessed it from the enthusiasm with which she began to kiss him. If she was trying to drive the memory of Amanda out of his head, that was fine with him. Jezebel's hot tongue thrust into his mouth and met his while she massaged his shaft with one hand. Her large breasts pushed against him, their nipples hard and hot.

When Jezebel finally came up for air, she didn't pause to catch her breath. She dove for Fargo's rigid tool and took it in her mouth sliding it in and out, tonguing it, and then almost swallowing it.

It was an amazing sensation, and Fargo thought he'd shoot right then. But Jezebel didn't let him. She raised up and straddled him. Crouched above him, she took his rod in one hand and guided it to her nether lips. She moved it back and forth, very slowly, at first just allowing the hair to tickle its sensitive tip. Then she slipped it inside herself and Fargo felt the tense pleasure bud as she rubbed him against it, gently, then harder in tiny circular motions.

Without warning, she lowered herself on him until he was completely engulfed. As she sat there, her head thrown back, he put his hands on her breasts with his palms over the nipples. He squeezed them and rolled them, and she started moving up and down on him. After a second, he found himself matching her motions, thrusting into her as she rose and then withdrawing to allow her to push down on him and envelop him once more.

She began to make small noises in the back of her throat, and Fargo was sure that she was going to wake everyone, but at that point he didn't care. Her breasts were engorged, and she started gasping.

"Ahhhhhh! Fargo! Fargo! Pleasssssse!"

Fargo didn't have to ask what she wanted since he couldn't have held back much longer even if he'd been made of iron. He erupted inside her, and her body trembled as her own climax rocked her, so much that she had to grab his shoulders in order to stay on him. Fargo shot again and again as Jezebel was wracked with the power of her own orgasm.

When she had stopped shaking, she lay atop him, completely relaxed. He thought for a second that she might be sleeping, but then she rolled aside.

He hadn't minded at all having her on top. It was different when a woman was doing it for your pleasure as much as her own. Amanda wouldn't have cared about him at all.

"You did like that, didn't you," Jezebel said. "I could tell."

"It was pretty obvious, I guess," Fargo said.

"I know you won't be staying on the island much longer," Jezebel told him. "But I'm glad I met you. I appreciate what you've done for us."

"I haven't done anything."

"Oh, but you have. You found the treasure, and you stood up to Gar Bollen and Sim Powell. You won't let them get away, either. I'm sure of that."

Fargo wished he was as sure as she seemed to be. He said, "Speaking of that, I guess we'd better get ready to go after Amanda. It's getting light outside."

"I'm sorry I disturbed your rest."

"I'm not," Fargo said.

21

Debris was everywhere.

Tree limbs and parts of rooftops were strewn in the streets and in yards. Dogs picked at bits of garbage, and cats worried at dead seabirds and small fish. Though some of the Gulf water had drained away, it still stood in pools and ran in rivulets. Horses wandered the streets and people filled their yards, talking loudly in the early morning light as they tried to decide where to begin making repairs.

The sun came up over the Gulf, cutting through the clouds and blazing across the now calm water. It was going to be a hot day in Galveston.

Fargo was wearing clothes that he had borrowed from Jed, who was almost as big as Fargo, but not quite. The clothes were an uncomfortable fit, but the day was already hot, and it was going to get hotter. Galveston was no place for buckskins.

"Coulda been worse, I guess," Carson said, speaking of the storm. "Probably nobody got killed unless they were caught away from any kind of shelter, or unless they went off into the storm on their own."

Fargo knew who Carson was thinking of, but he didn't believe Bollen, Powell, or Amanda had been killed. That would have been too convenient. He wasn't too sure about Ben, but if he was dead it wouldn't be the storm that had killed him.

"You sure this is a good idea?" Carson asked.

"You have a better one?" Fargo asked.

"Guess not. Might's well give it a try."

Fargo's idea was simple. Amanda would know that getting off the island would be next to impossible for several days. She had a way of being very convincing, and Fargo thought she would be able to bring Powell and Bollen around to her

138

way of thinking. Ben would be no problem at all. So what Fargo had to do was decide just what her way of thinking would be.

He'd decided she'd be thinking of revenge, on him maybe, but almost certainly on Jezebel and Carson.

And the most likely place for her to hide out? Where no one would ever think to look for her and where she would also stand a good chance of getting the revenge she was looking for.

"I still don't see why she'd go to my place," Carson said.

He and Fargo were riding two "borrowed" horses. They had no idea who the horses belonged to, but they could return them to town later if they survived the encounter that Fargo believed was ahead of them.

"She'd go there because she thinks that sooner or later, you and Jezebel will show up. She can set up an ambush for you and just wait for you to walk into it."

"That sounds like her, all right," Jezebel said. "But what if you're wrong?"

She and Jed were riding in a buckboard that Jed had rented at a livery stable. The stable hadn't been damaged at all in the storm, and Jed had been able to rent a horse to pull the buckboard as well.

"If I'm wrong we'll have to think of something else," Fargo said, but he didn't think he was wrong. Going to Carson's place was the logical thing for Amanda to do. The ranch was at the nearly deserted western end of the island, which made it a good place to hide out for a while, and if Amanda could engineer the deaths of Jezebel and Carson, she would be that much happier. No one would miss them for days, not with all the confusion caused by the storm in town. No one would be interested in checking on that end of the island for a good while, and after a little time had passed, Bollen and Powell could leave the island with their gold.

Fargo was sure that Amanda had never really cared about the gold. Getting hold of it was just a way to hurt Jezebel, and Amanda wouldn't mind letting Bollen and Powell have it. She had a house and a brother and a position in the society of the island. She would believe she could go back to things the way they'd always been. Why should she leave the island?

139

Though Fargo didn't know what story she would feed Jed to persuade him that she'd never done anything wrong, he was sure she could cook one up. And with Jezebel out of the way, Amanda would have Jed all to herself again.

As for Ben, Fargo didn't hold out much hope for his survival. He was just one of Amanda's puppets, and she'd cut his strings without a second thought.

"I hope the cattle got through the storm," Jezebel said, interrupting Fargo's thoughts.

"You can bet those critters sheltered in the trees and dunes," Carson said. "And if there's a piece of ground an inch above the water this morning, they're standing on it. Trouble is, the salt water will probably kill most of the grass, and it'll ruin the fresh water supplies for sure. We'll have to take care of that pretty quick. That is, if we don't all get shot to pieces in this ambush Fargo thinks is waiting for us."

"I still find it hard to believe that Amanda would have a part in something like that," Jed said.

That was the trouble with people like Jed, Fargo thought. They could never believe that someone close to them could go bad. But it happened all the time. Gar Bollen and Sim Powell had been somebody's cute little babies once, just like Amanda had.

"She really had no reason to be jealous of you, Jezebel," Jed went on. "I would never have turned her out of our home, even if you'd married me." He paused, then said, "I don't suppose you could ever see your way clear to allowing me to call on you, now that you're going to be a wealthy woman."

"We don't know I'm going to be wealthy," Jezebel said. "We don't have the gold yet. If Fargo's wrong, it might already be off the island."

Fargo noticed that Jezebel hadn't exactly answered Jed's question, but he wasn't sure Jed had noticed.

"This place sure looks different," Carson said, changing the subject. "Nothing like a storm to make you realize that nothing lasts forever."

They were riding along what yesterday had been a rutted road not far from the beach. Now, there was no beach to be seen. The water was too high and there were no waves now. The water was wide and nearly flat under a clear blue sky that looked as if it had never seen a cloud. There was seaweed spread over the dunes, but much of the vegetation that had grown on them had been ripped away and blown across the island. The ruts of the sandy road were washed away and it was difficult for the horses to pull the buckboard along the slushy sand. The horses Carson and Fargo rode picked their way and often managed to put their hooves on places that were out of the water. Sometimes, when they picked up their feet, there would be a sucking sound as wet sand and water filled the vacuum left behind.

Overhead, the seagulls wheeled and cried. They would be the ones to profit from the storm. There were lots of dead crabs and fish around, and the gulls would feed on them for days. Now there was no smell, but Fargo knew that in a day or so, it would be quite fragrant all over the island.

"Gotta be careful of snakes," Carson said, looking things over. "The high water drives 'em out of their holes."

"What kind of snakes?" Fargo asked.

"Rattlers. They're all over the island, but you don't see 'em much unless there's a storm or a big rain."

Fargo hoped they didn't run into any rattlers. He wasn't overly fond of snakes.

When they came to the oak trees where the treasure had been buried, Carson glanced at them wistfully.

"Just think," he said. "I had Lafitte's treasure in my hands, and it got away from me."

"You'll have it again," Fargo said, trying to sound more confident than he felt.

Carson grinned ruefully behind his scraggly beard.

"I hope you're right about that," he said.

"We don't really need the gold anymore," Jezebel said. "Now that we know Jed wasn't trying to take the ranch, we don't need the money to fight him."

"You never needed it to fight me," Jed said. "I'd never do the kinds of things you say Amanda did."

"Never hurts to have money, just in case," Carson said. "Comes in handy, now and then."

The sun was well up into the sky. It gave the water a coppery color, and to Fargo the steamy heat seemed to rise up out of the ground and surround them. Fargo's borrowed clothes were soaked with sweat, and they hung as heavily on him as if they'd been drenched by the storm.

Tiny black mosquitos swarmed out of the dunes and attacked any bit of exposed skin. Fargo heard their humming in both ears as he brushed them away from his face.

"We're not all that far from the house," Carson said after a while. "I hope you know what you're talking about, Fargo."

Fargo hoped the same thing. His plan was simple. He and Carson would ride as wide as they could of the house, in order to stay out of sight of anyone hiding inside. Jed and Jezebel would give them a chance to come up behind the house, then continue in the buckboard and let themselves be seen. Fargo thought that seeing Jed would confuse Amanda and any of the others long enough for Fargo and Carson to get the drop on them. Assuming there was no one watching the back of the house.

"I don't like the idea of exposing Jezebel to danger," Jed said.

Fargo didn't like it, either. So he said, "I think she should get out of the buckboard right now. Amanda won't shoot you, but she might shoot Jezebel."

"And all the rest of them will shoot Jed," Jezebel said. "I'm going with him."

"The hell you are," Carson said. "You may be a woman grown, but you're still my daughter, and you still have to do what I tell you."

"I haven't been doing that since I was six," Jezebel said. "Unless what you told me to do was what I wanted to do in the first place. So there's no use in you talking. I'm going with Jed."

Fargo noticed that Jed was sitting a little straighter in the buckboard. He probably thought he had a chance with Jezebel after all. For all Fargo knew, he could have been right. The signs seemed to be pointing that way.

"We'll do what we can," Fargo said. "If anyone starts shooting, get out of the buckboard and take cover."

Jezebel nodded, and Carson and Fargo rode away.

* * *

142

Some of Carson's cattle were gathered on a little rise that stood above the water. Others were under some oak trees surrounded by a mound that rose up over its roots.

"Some of 'em are around the barn, too," Carson said. "It's higher there, but not much."

They could see the back of the house, still surrounded by brush, though some of the bushes had been torn away.

"Reckon there's anybody in there?" Carson asked.

"We'll find out," Fargo said. "Let's ride a little closer. Then we'll get off the horses and walk."

They rode for another fifty yards before coming to a stop. Fargo could make out the buckboard as it headed toward the house.

"There they are," Fargo said, slipping off his mount. "If there's going to be shooting it'll start soon. Come on."

There wasn't much cover, so Fargo moved as low to the ground as he could. Carson couldn't bend over as far or move as fast, but he was game and managed to keep up fairly well. He was armed with a pistol that Jed had given him, and Fargo had his Colt.

They hadn't gone far before the shooting began. The buckboard didn't slow down, and no one got out of it. For a second or two, Fargo couldn't figure out what was happening.

"What the hell?" Carson asked.

Fargo shrugged. He didn't have an answer.

There was more shooting, and this time the horse pulling the buckboard reared up. Fargo watched as Jed pulled back on the reins, got the horse under control, and somehow managed to turn its head back toward town.

Fargo and Carson ran toward the back of the house. When they got there, Fargo threw the door open and went into the kitchen. There was no one there, but the gold was stacked on the table.

"Stay here," Fargo told Carson, and ran to the front door.

He took in the scene quickly. Ben lay face down on the ground. Bollen was firing at the fleeing buckboard, and Sim Powell had one arm around a struggling Amanda, who was kicking at his shins and screaming.

Fargo didn't know what warned Powell, but some animal

instinct in the man must have been on the alert, for he suddenly turned and saw Fargo.

He didn't waste any time trying to shoot. He simply put his pistol to Amanda's head and said, "Take another step and I'll kill her."

Bollen turned around at Powell's words. When he saw Fargo, he grinned.

"You out-figured us, Fargo. I told the little lady we shoulda gone for the railroad."

"It wouldn't have worked," Fargo said.

"Don't matter. We got the better of you here. You just back off now, and we'll go inside for the gold. Either that or we put a hole in her head."

"Go ahead," Fargo said.

Bollen's grin faded. Amanda stopped struggling in Powell's arms and stared at Fargo.

"She doesn't mean a thing to me," Fargo said. "Go on and kill her."

"You must be crazy," Amanda said.

"It's been said before," Fargo told her.

"They've already killed Ben," Amanda said. "And all he tried to do was warn Jed."

"More likely he was trying to warn Jezebel," Fargo said.

Amanda's mouth twisted in an ugly grimace.

"He didn't care a thing about that cow," she said. "Not any more. Not after he'd had me."

Fargo didn't bother to contradict her. Let her believe what she wanted to believe. Maybe it would make things easier for her when she died.

Because Fargo had been telling the truth. Amanda meant nothing to him, as hard as it was for her to believe that. If Powell shot her, it might give Fargo a chance to jump him, and right now he'd take any chance he could get.

"You could be right," Fargo said.

"I *am* right."

Fargo shrugged. Looking beyond her, he could see that Jed had the wagon turned again and was coming back. He wished Jed had just kept on going toward town.

Bollen must have noticed something in Fargo's eyes. He turned and saw the wagon, too.

"Looks like big brother wants to save his little sister," Bollen said. "We'll let him get closer, and then can kill 'em both."

"Fargo, too," Powell said.

"Him first," Bollen replied.

22

Amanda squirmed in Powell's arms and bit him. She sank her teeth into his sweat-soaked shirt near the shoulder and clamped down, twisting her head and trying, or so it seemed to Fargo, to tear out a chunk of meat the size of a good steak.

Powell howled in pain and surprise. He squeezed off two shots, both of which went into the ground at his feet.

Fargo was already reaching for his own pistol before Powell's first shot went wild. He shot Powell in the shoulder that Amanda had bitten. Powell released Amanda, who fell writhing to the ground, where she screamed and kicked at his ankles.

Powell, however, knew where the real danger was. He ignored her and brought up his pistol. It didn't rise very far because Fargo shot him twice in the chest, the holes less than a finger's width apart.

Powell fell beside Amanda, who snatched his pistol from his suddenly limp fingers. Holding the gun in both hands, she turned and began shooting in the direction of Bollen, who was running toward the buckboard.

Fargo stepped over to her and slapped the pistol out of her hands.

"You'll kill Jed," he said.

It would have been an accident if she hit anyone at all, considering the distance Bollen had covered, but it was better not to take any chances. Fargo left Amanda sitting there and started after Bollen.

Bollen wasn't firing, either. Jed was driving the buckboard straight for him, and Bollen stood rigidly as if waiting for it to run over him.

That wasn't his plan, and Fargo knew it, but he couldn't

warn Jed, who wouldn't have been able to hear him even if he'd yelled.

Bollen waited until the buckboard was almost on him, then jumped to the side.

But not far. He grabbed the harness as the horse went by him and swung up on its back. Jed pulled the long, thin whip from its place and lashed at Bollen with it, but Bollen just laughed. He got hold of the whip and pulled it, hard.

Jed should have let go, but he didn't. He was jerked from his seat and fell under the buckboard, which passed over him without hitting him.

The reins had fallen from his hands when he dropped to the ground, and Bollen was now in control. He turned the buckboard aside and headed it off across the island.

Fargo thought Jezebel might jump from the seat, but she didn't. Bollen was kicking his heels into the horse's sides, and the buckboard was going too fast for Jezebel to do much more than simply hang on. She sat gripping the seat with both hands as they bounced away.

"Let them go," Amanda said from behind Fargo. "Who cares about her?"

"I do," Carson said.

He was standing beside Amanda. He had run from the house when the shooting began, but he didn't appear to know what to do to stop Bollen's escape.

"To hell with you, old man," Amanda said. "Who cares about you, either."

She picked up Powell's pistol. Then she got to her feet and ran to where Jed lay.

Fargo stayed where he was, waiting to see what Bollen would do. He knew Bollen wasn't leaving. The gold was still inside the house, and Bollen wanted it. He wouldn't be able to just leave it there, not after all he'd gone through to get his hands on it in the first place.

To get it again, however, he had to go through Fargo. He turned the buckboard and started in Fargo's direction.

Bollen lay low on the horse's back and fired as he got closer. He missed.

Fargo didn't return the fire because he was afraid he might

147

hit Jezebel. She was still sitting upright in the seat, and a stray bullet could easily kill her.

Bollen didn't care who got hit, and he fired again. Carson went down without a sound, but Fargo was sure Bollen had been trying for him instead.

Before he got too near Fargo, Bollen veered off and rode away. If he'd gotten much closer, Fargo could have risked a shot.

Fargo thought that if he could get Carson inside before Bollen tried again to kill them, they might have a chance. If Carson wasn't dead already.

Fargo knelt by Carson, who was breathing heavily. He'd been hit by a bullet that had creased his scalp and knocked him unconscious. There was a lot of blood, but Fargo didn't think he was in any danger of dying.

He grabbed Carson under the arms and hauled him up off the ground. The old man was heavier than he looked.

"Fargo!" Amanda said. "You have to help me with Jed."

Fargo glanced over at the two of them. Jed was sitting up and appeared dazed, but he couldn't have been hurt as badly as Carson was, so Fargo ignored Amanda and started to drag Carson into the house.

A shot from Bollen stopped him.

"You forgetting about the woman, Fargo?" Bollen yelled from the back of the horse.

Fargo hadn't forgotten. He'd hoped that Jezebel might have jumped when Bollen slowed down. He looked over at the buckboard, which Bollen had brought to a stop out of the Colt's range.

It was as if Jezebel were reading his mind. She lunged from the buckboard and started to run.

She was smart. She didn't run in a straight line but in a weaving path that would make it hard for Bollen to hit her. But she was having a hard time running in the wet sand, and Bollen must have thought he could hit her.

As it turned out, he got lucky. His first shot spun her around in her tracks. She looked at Fargo and opened her mouth as if she were going to say something, but she didn't get it out before falling.

"Serves the bitch right," Amanda said. "Why don't you help her, Fargo?"

Fargo believed in cutting his losses. If Jezebel was dead, there was nothing he could do for her. If she wasn't, he'd do something later. He started for the house again.

He was almost there when he saw Jed stand up. And when Jed saw that Jezebel had been shot, he started walking unsteadily in her direction.

For a second or so, Fargo thought Amanda might shoot him, but she didn't. There was no way she could do that, not even to stop him from helping Jezebel. She watched him take a couple of steps before she turned her back on him and walked toward the house.

Fargo got Carson inside and laid him on the floor. The old man's breathing was still strong, so Fargo went back outside.

Amanda was standing by the door, looking at her brother, who was kneeling over Jezebel. She was holding Powell's pistol down at her side in her right hand.

"I hope she's dead," Amanda said.

"You might get your wish," Fargo said, pointing to Bollen, still lying low on the horse's back as it pulled the buckboard toward Jed. "Or he might just decide to kill your brother. I don't think Bollen cares who he kills."

Amanda raised the pistol she was holding, gripped it in both hands and fired.

Fargo thought she was just wasting ammunition, but then he realized that she wasn't shooting at Bollen.

She was shooting at the horse.

The gun jumped in her hands, but she lowered it and fired again. And again.

Fargo didn't know how many times she hit the horse. Maybe all three times. The animal stopped, staggered to the right, and fell. Bollen managed to jump off its back just in time, rolling away across the sand.

Fargo went after him, firing twice on the run, although he knew he'd be unlikely to hit him.

Bollen sprang to his feet and fired back, but neither shot came close. He holstered his pistol and started to run through the puddles that dotted the sand.

When Fargo passed Jezebel and Jed, Jed looked up and said, "She's alive, but we have to get the bleeding stopped."

"You do it," Fargo said. "Call Amanda for help. I have to catch Bollen."

Fargo couldn't just let the man go. If he got away, he'd plague the Carsons until he killed them or they killed him, and Fargo wasn't sure Bollen would care which.

Bollen ran behind a dune, and Fargo slowed down. The way he figured it, Bollen had one more shot, the same as Fargo. Fargo didn't want to get caught by surprise.

At the same time, he didn't want to give Bollen a chance to reload. He decided to try to spring a surprise of his own. Instead of going around the dune, he went over the top.

The sand shifted beneath his feet, and Fargo was sure that Bollen could hear him coming, but it was too late to turn back. He crested the dune, his pistol ready.

Bollen stood there, and he was ready, too, his gun pointed right at Fargo.

Fargo stopped and looked down at him.

"Well, Fargo, wonder which one of us it's gonna be?" Bollen said, thumbing back the hammer of his pistol. "I figure it's you."

Bollen didn't look scared. He didn't even look worried. His hat was pushed back, and Fargo could see the mad light in his eyes.

He should have been worried, and scared too, but not because of Fargo.

"Don't step backward, Bollen," Fargo told him. "Or you'll be in real trouble."

"You must be really scared of dying to try that one, Fargo."

"I'm not trying anything," Fargo said. "Just stand still and quiet and listen. You'll hear something in a second."

Bollen tried a grin, but it slipped off his face when he heard the buzzing of the rattler behind him. It was about five feet long, Fargo thought. Thicker than a man's arm. There was an even longer one not far off, but it hadn't coiled itself up into striking position yet. It didn't look too happy, though.

"I'll be damned," Bollen said.

"I figure we can pretty well count on that," Fargo told him.

The other rattler coiled around and raised its ugly head. The hum of its rattle was more impressive than that of the smaller snake's.

"You shoot that pistol, and they'll strike," Fargo said.

"Maybe," Bollen said. "Maybe not."

"I'm betting they will."

"You have a bullet left, Fargo. So do I. You get one, I get the other."

"What happens then?"

"We'd just have to find out."

"I don't think so," Fargo said. "Besides, who'd take the other two?"

Two more rattlers crawled out of a small pile of driftwood near Bollen's right foot, their rattles vibrating. It seemed to Fargo that they were even angrier than the other two. All Bollen had to do was move, and they'd all strike. At least one of them was bound to get him. Maybe they all would. Another one emerged from the wood.

"Shit," Bollen said.

That pretty much summed it up, Fargo thought.

"They're not mad at you," he said. "They're heated up because the flood ran them out of their home."

"Not a hell of a lot of difference, is there," Bollen said.

"You can shoot one of them and try to reload," Fargo said. "Or you could run. You might have a chance. I'll leave you to it."

"You bastard," Bollen said, but Fargo hardly heard him. He was already walking back down the side of the dune.

He heard a shot from the other side, and then all he could hear was Bollen's screams.

Fargo walked back to where Jed was working on Jezebel. He had taken her shirt off and ripped up his own shirt to make a bandage for her side. He hadn't asked for help from Amanda.

Jezebel was sitting up and trying to smile, but she wasn't doing a very good job of it.

"How's my father?" she asked.

"He's resting," Fargo said. "He'll be all right. What about you?"

"Took a little bit of flesh out of her side, but not much," Jed said. "I think it might have grazed a rib, though. Probably cracked it."

"Hurts like hell," Jezebel told Fargo. "I hope you killed Bollen."

"I didn't," Fargo said. "I let some rattlers do the job. He might not be dead yet, but it won't be long."

There was silence from behind the dune now. Fargo thought of Bollen lying there and bloating up in the sun from the poison. The thought didn't bother him any.

"Can you walk?" he asked Jezebel.

"I can try."

She got to her feet with Jed's help, biting her lower lip to keep from crying out.

"You'll have to bind those ribs up for a while," Fargo said. "Sooner or later, they'll feel better. Think you can walk to the house?"

"I guess so."

"You can lean on me," Jed said, putting an arm around her waist.

Fargo wasn't sure that Jezebel needed much help, but she leaned into Jed, letting him have a feel of her generous breasts. Fargo had a feeling that Jezebel had changed her mind about some things. Maybe the island was big enough for her after all. And maybe she was going to give Jed a chance. Jed seemed to sense the change. He was looking a lot happier than he had at any time since Fargo had met him.

Amanda wasn't looking happy at all. She came out of the shade of the house and walked toward them, still holding the pistol.

"Jed, we have to go now," she said. "It's time for us to get back to the house and set things right."

Jed stood up a little straighter. He said, "We can't go back now. We don't have any way to get there except to walk. Anyway, the house was just fine when we left. The Carsons are the ones who need help setting things right."

"They have help."

Jed looked over to where Ben lay.

"No, they don't," he said. "And it's your fault. You've gotten so many people killed that I've lost count. At least Ben figured out what was right before he died. I'm not sure you've figured anything out. What about Isaiah? If there's any reason to go home, it's to help Lucinda with his funeral."

"He was just an old darkie," Amanda said.

"An old darkie who raised you," Jed told her. "But then I don't think you've ever cared about anyone except yourself."

"You can't say that!" Amanda told him. "I care about *you!* Everything I do is for you. Can't you see that?"

"No," Jed said. "I can't. What have you ever done for me, or for anybody?"

Maybe Amanda had an answer for that, but Fargo never found out because that was when Gar Bollen showed up again.

Bollen staggered out from behind the dune. His face was a terrible shade of gray, and there was a rattler hanging from his lower leg. The snake's fangs were stuck in Bollen's calf, and the snake twisted in a frenzy as it tried to let go.

"Shoot me," Bollen said. "For God's sake, Fargo. Shoot me."

Fargo thought about it, but Amanda acted.

Her first shot hit him in the stomach.

The next one was higher and took him in the chest. Bollen sank down on his knees, then pitched forward on his face.

"See?" Amanda said, looking first at Jed and then at Fargo. "I did something for him."

"I'm sure he appreciates it," Fargo said.

Jed took Jezebel back to the house, though she didn't seem to Fargo to need the help. Then Jed went back outside to talk to Amanda. Carson was leaning against a wall. The scalp wound was still oozing blood, but it didn't look too bad to Fargo.

"What happened?" Carson asked. "Did I get kicked by a mule?"

"You got shot," Fargo said. "So did Jezebel, but you'll both be all right. Turns out your head is just as hard as mine."

"Glad to hear it. There's a jug of whiskey under my bed, Fargo. Bring it in here, will you?"

Fargo located the jug and took it to Carson, who uncorked it and took a hefty swig.

"I feel better already," he said, wiping his mouth on his

sleeve. "Now dab some of this stuff on my head and put a bandage on it."

Fargo did what he was told and then cleaned Jezebel's wound and rebandaged it with clean cloth. He bound the ribs tightly, which helped with the pain.

"What about you and Jed?" he asked when he was done.

"That's up to Jed. I think he's changed a lot today. I believe he's going to stand up to Amanda and lead his own life. If he does, well, we'll see."

"They're still out there arguing," Fargo said. "He's giving her hell."

"Not as much as she deserves," Jezebel said. "She should suffer for what she's done."

"She will," Fargo said. "I think you and Jed will see to that."

"What's all the yelling about, anyhow?" Carson asked.

"Just a family fight," Fargo told him. "Nothing to worry about."

"Good. You want to hang around the place for a while, Fargo? Help me get things running again? We can decide just how much of that gold I owe you for what you've already done."

"And you never know," Jezebel said. "Jed might not work out, after all."

Fargo admired the rise of her bosom.

"That's right," he said. "You never can tell."

LOOKING FORWARD!

**The following is the opening
section from the next novel in the exciting
Trailsman series from Signet:**

**THE TRAILSMAN #247
SEVEN DEVILS SLAUGHTER**

*Seven Devils country, 1861—Evil comes in human
guise, snaring the innocent deep among its dark hills.*

Skye Fargo liked to play poker as much as the next man. He
liked the challenge, the thrill of pitting his wits against others
in a high-stakes contest. But one thing he didn't like was a
cardsharp, or card mechanics as they were known. Tinhorns
who cheated rather than play fair. Men who thought they were
as slick as axle grease and went about fleecing tenderfeet and
wide-eyed fools.

Fargo was no greenhorn, and he sure as hell was no fool.
He was a big, broad-shouldered man with piercing lake-blue
eyes and the muscular grace of a mountain lion in the way he
moved and held himself. He favored buckskins and boots and
a red bandanna, and strapped around his lean waist was a Colt,
its grips worn smooth from regular use. Now, as he stared
across the table at the polecat who was cheating, his blue eyes
lit with an inner fire no one else noticed. He kept a poker face
as he watched the man rake in the pot, then slid his cards toward the dealer.

"Yes, sir," the card cheat crowed, his porcine face aglow

with greed. "Lady Luck has been sitting in my lap this whole game."

"And here I thought you were pregnant," quipped a player to Fargo's left. He was tall and lean and wore a black frock coat, a white shirt, and a black hat tilted low over his dark eyes. Unless Fargo missed his guess, the tall drink of water was a professional gambler, and like him, had spotted the heavyset cardsharp's sleight of hand.

The cheat glanced down at his ample belly, and frowned. "I don't much like having folks poke fun at my expense, Denton." His clothes were as slovenly as he was, and consisted of a cheap suit, a bowler smeared with grime, and a shirt that served as a catchall for food that missed his mouth. But there was nothing cheap about the Smith and Wesson buckled to his left hip. It was the latest model, clean and well-oiled.

The gambler smiled thinly and responded, "I don't much care what you like, Mr. Swill. And I'll thank you not to use that tone with me ever again." As he spoke, he rested his right arm on the table.

Fargo heard the scrape of metal on wood. It was obvious that the gambler had a derringer up his sleeve. Swill realized it, too, and flushed with resentment but didn't say anything more.

"Gentlemen, gentlemen, please!" declared the dealer. His name was Harry Barnes and he owned the ramshackle excuse for a saloon. The only watering hole in the small settlement of Les Bois, it boasted a plank counter for a bar, four tables that needed new legs, and chairs that creaked when those seated in them so much as twitched. "This is supposed to be a friendly game. Let's not have any trouble."

"Fine by me," Swill said.

The last two players, both locals, bobbed their heads in agreement, and one of them cast a sly look at Swill.

Only then did Fargo catch on that the game itself was rigged. The card mechanic wasn't playing alone. Swill had partners. Among the gambling fraternity, it was known as a card mob. Fargo had a hunch all three local men were in on it.

Not Barnes, though. The owner played too ineptly. A friendly old cuss who had opened the saloon as much to satisfy his own craving for liquor as anything else, he was also a chatterbox.

Barnes began gathering in the rest of the cards. A half-empty bottle of rotgut was perched next to his elbow, and every so often he would take a healthy swig. Now, pausing, he lifted the bottle to his mouth, gulped a few times, smacked his grizzled lips, and sighed with contentment. "I sure am glad you boys happened by," he said to Fargo and the gambler. "Other than an occasional wagon train off the Oregon Trail, we don't see all that many new faces here."

Fargo could see why. Les Bois was well off the beaten path. Founded by a French-Canadian trapper who gave the place its name, the settlement was situated near the Boise River. It was literally in the middle of nowhere, miles north and east of the Oregon Trail. Even calling it a settlement was giving it more credit than it was due. It consisted of the saloon, a stable, and a sorry excuse for a general store. That was all. There were no homes, no families. Not in town, at any rate. Most of the locals were backwoods sorts. Hunters and trappers, men who lived off the land. Recluses who shunned human company. Outcasts who wanted nothing to do with civilization or its trappings; unsavory types like Swill and his partners, who weren't above trying to fleece a couple of travelers.

Fargo sat back and took a sip of whiskey. He was on his second glass and his gut was pleasantly warm. And empty. He had been on the go most of the day and stopped over in Les Bois on a whim. Soon the sun would set and he would have to find a spot to bed down for the night. Tomorrow he would move on, bound for the Pacific Coast.

Barnes began dealing. The deck was in front of him, and he flipped the cards off the top slowly, one by one, exaggerating his movements so no one could accuse him of anything shady. Glancing at Fargo, he remarked, "You haven't mentioned your name yet, friend."

"Are you sure?"

Barnes blinked, then chortled. "I get it. That's your way of telling me to mind my own business." He slid a card across. "I'm not trying to be nosy, mister. I just see no reason to sit here like a bunch of tree stumps."

Swill made a sniffing sound. "Hell, Harry, you prattle like a woman at times. I swear, it's enough to drive a gent to drink." He guffawed loudly and was joined by the other two locals.

Harry Barnes stiffened, then said something peculiar. "You would know all about women, wouldn't you, Gus?"

To Fargo's surprise, the cheat came half out of his chair and his left hand dropped to his Smith and Wesson.

Swill's jowls worked and his cheeks puffed out like those of a riled squirrel. For a few seconds it appeared he would draw, but instead he merely glowered and eased back down. "You ought to keep a rein on that tongue of yours, Harry. It'll be the death of you one day if you're not mighty careful."

The other two locals were also glaring. Barnes shriveled under their gaze, then forced a grin and tried to lighten the mood by saying, "You know me, boys. Always gabbing away. No one ever takes me seriously."

"You'd best hope to God they don't," Swill said.

Fargo's curiosity was aroused. The saloon owner's comment hardly merited such hostility. "There must be a shortage of women in these parts," he mentioned to see how they'd react.

Swill and the others clammed up. Swill pretended to be interested in his filthy fingernails and the other two just stared at the table.

Only Barnes responded. "Ain't that the truth, friend. Most feminine critters don't cotton to living in the wilds. They like a nice home and pretty dresses and all that foofaraw. Not a one-room cabin off in the sticks." He nodded toward the bar. "Mabel, there, is fixing to move on to San Francisco just as soon as she saves up a couple of hundred dollars."

"Which shouldn't take her more than five or ten years," Swill threw in, and he and his friend chortled.

Mabel was the sole female inhabitant of Les Bois. In her

late twenties, she had red hair that she wasn't fussy about keeping brushed, and a pretty face on which she dabbed more war paint than ten Sioux warriors combined. She wore a tight red dress that clung to her like a second layer of skin. A couple of minutes ago she had strayed over to the bar to refill her glass. She heard Swill's comment, and as she sashayed back she said, "What do you know, you dunderhead? One more year in this flea-ridden dive should do it." She halted beside Fargo's chair and brushed his shoulder with her painted nails. "What about you, handsome? Care to treat a lady to a few drinks later?"

Fargo was the last man in the world to ever refuse female company. "See me later," he said. At the moment he couldn't afford to be distracted from the game.

The cards had been dealt. Everyone was contemplating their hands. Fargo had two kings, a queen, a seven, and a three. Swill opened, indicating he had a pair or better. Fargo stayed in, and when his turn came to ask for more cards, he requested two. He held onto the queen on the chance he might get another. He didn't, but he did receive another king and a four of clubs.

Swill had a good hand, too—or so he tried to convince everyone by raising the stakes. Barnes and the other locals bowed out.

Fargo stayed in.

"That's ten dollars to you, friend," Swill said to the gambler. "Unless you'd rather be smart and get out while you still have a shirt on your back."

Denton's thin lips curled in contempt. "I reckon I'll keep playing, Mr. Swill. I aim to see this through to the end."

"Your choice," Swill said, shrugging. And as he shrugged, he slid one of his cards up his right sleeve and replaced it with a card from up under his left. He was quick, Fargo had to hand him that. But he lacked the nimble finesse needed to be a truly good cardsharp. "Just don't hold it against me if I don't feel a bit guilty taking your money."

"Not at all," Denton said, shifting his right arm so his hand was pointed in Swill's direction. "Provided you won't hold it against me if I buck you out in gore for giving card slicks a bad name."

"How's that?" Swill asked. He had gone rigid, and the other two locals had the look of ten-years-olds whose hands had been caught in a cookie jar.

"I've run into a lot of cheats in my time," Denton went on. "You're not the worst, but you're damn close to it. You should never try the same trick two hands in a row. That's the mark of an amateur."

Swill slowly pushed his chair back. "Talk like that can get a man killed, gambler."

"So can cheating," Denton said.

One of the other locals chimed in, a brawny specimen in dire need of a bath. "We know Gus Swill real well, mister. He'd never cheat anyone. He's as honest as the year is long."

The gambler grinned. "And you're a bald-faced liar."

Their bluff had been called. Fargo expected them to try for their hardware and they didn't disappoint him. Swill was fastest, but the Smith and Wesson wasn't clear of its holster before Fargo pushed to his feet and filled his hand with his Colt. As he drew he thumbed back the hammer, and at the loud *click* the three locals turned to stone.

Simultaneously, Denton had given his right wrist a flick and a Remington-Eliot .32-caliber four-barrel derringer had slidden into his palm. Commonly known as a pepperbox, it had a ring trigger and was quite deadly at short range.

Fargo sidled around the table to come up on Swill from behind. Reaching under the cheat's arm, he relieved Swill of the Smith and Wesson and slid it off across the floor. Then he gripped the wide cuff of Swill's left sleeve, and tugged upward. It rose high enough to reveal a mechanical holdout strapped to Swill's forearm. A similar tug on Swill's other sleeve revealed a second holdout.

"Talk about greedy," Denton said, rising. "What should we do with these jackasses, friend? The last town I was in, they hung a card sharp from the most convenient tree. And I noticed plenty of trees outside."

Harry Barnes stood and hastily stepped back. "I want you boys to know I had no part in this. I've never swindled a soul in all my born days."

"I'll vouch for that," Mabel said, and treated herself to a more than healthy swallow of rotgut.

Fargo frisked Swill and found a Green River knife, which he tossed into a corner. "Your turn now," he told the cheat's companions, and took a step toward them.

Demonstrating he had more sinew than brains, the brawny tough yelled, "Like hell!" He heaved out of his chair and made a mad grab for a Volcanic Arms brass-plated pistol tucked under his belt.

Fargo lunged, and brought the Colt's barrel crashing down onto the bridge of the man's nose. Cartilage crunched. Blood spurted over the tough's cheeks and jaw as he drew up short, howling in outrage as much as pain.

Fargo relieved him of the pistol, then stepped back. The third man opened his jacket and turned completely around to show he wasn't heeled. Motioning for them to move well back, Fargo faced the main culprit.

Gus Swill was white as high country snow. Beads of sweat had sprouted on his sloping brow, and he nervously licked his pudgy lips. "Don't do anything hasty, mister! Why don't you take the pot and all my winnings and we'll call it even? Divide it up with the gambler, if you like."

"I was planning on doing that anyway," Fargo said. He leveled the Colt at the portly man's ample stomach.

"Don't!" Swill whined, his nerve breaking. "What I did was wrong, sure, but no harm came of it."

Denton came around the table. "Only because we caught you before you walked off with our money, you obscene slug." He jammed the muzzles of the pepperpot against Swill's temple and Swill bleated like a terror-struck goat. "I would be perfectly in my rights to blow a hole in your head."

"Hold on!" Swill cried shrilly. "It ain't right to kill a man over a little thing like cards."

"A little thing?" Denton repeated coldly. "I'll have you know cards are how I make my living. You've not only slandered my profession, you've insulted every honorable gambler alive."

Fargo repressed a grin. Honesty and gambling hardly went hand-in-hand. The simple fact was, most gamblers cheated in some form or another. Some relied on sleight of hand. Others used rings or poker chips with tiny mirrors on them to read cards. Still others preferred marked decks. Then there were those, like Swill, whose fingers weren't nimble enough to deal crookedly without the aid of a holdout.

Swill nervously wiped a sleeve across his forehead. "What is it you want from me? Ask anything and it's yours. My horse. My saddle. My belongings."

"For starters, we'll dispose of your toys," Denton said, and tapped the pepperbox against the holdout on Swill's right forearm.

"Have a heart," Swill said plaintively. "I sent for these from a mail-order outfit. Do you have any notion how much they cost?"

Fargo had seen some of the advertisements in newspapers and on flyers posted in saloons all over the West. The premier supplier of "advantage tools," as they were commonly referred to, was prestigious Grandine's of New York City. Grandine's put out an entire catalogue of nothing but marked cards, holdouts, doctored dice, card trimmers, phosphorescent ink, and specially tinted blue glasses to read cards marked with the ink. None of the items were cheap. A single holdout of the kind worn by Swill cost upwards of twenty-five dollars.

"Consider it a lesson learned," Denton said, and wagged the pepperbox. "Shuck them or I'll relieve you of your ears."

"You wouldn't!" Swill blustered.

Denton's left arm flicked and a dagger materialized in his hand. "A riverboat cheat once said the same thing. They call him One-eared Tom now."

Swill sullenly hiked his sleeve higher and began to undo the leather straps that held the holdout in place.

Harry Barnes had retreated to the sanctuary of his bar, while Mabel stood there sipping her drink and grinning at Swill's expense. "What are your brothers going to say when they hear how you crawled?" she taunted.

"Shut up, bitch," Swill snapped, his eyes twin barbs of spite.

"Or what? You'll beat on me like I hear you do that poor filly of yours?" Mabel snorted. "I'd like to see you try. I'll turn you from a steer into a heifer."

Swill started to rise but stopped when Denton jabbed the dagger against his neck. "I won't forget this," he rasped at her. "My brothers and me will pay you a visit one of these nights."

"I'm real scared," Mabel said, and laughed. "Lay a finger on me and you'll have every male from here to Canada out for your blood. As the only fancy-free and easy gal within a hundred miles, I'm right popular. Or haven't you noticed?"

"That she is," Barnes interjected. "Harm a hair on her head and there will be hell to pay."

Swill finished with the straps and smacked the holdout down onto the table. "You don't fool anyone, old man. The only reason you care is because you get ten percent of her take. If you lose her, you know damn well you won't find another woman crazy enough to stay in Les Bois." Then he added, almost as an afterthought, "Not willingly, anyhow."

"Enough jabbering," Fargo broke in. He was tired of listening to Swill flap his gums. He had been keeping the other two covered while the gambler covered Swill, but now he turned to the cheat and jabbed the end of the Colt's barrel into Swill's keg of a gut. "If I hear you've hurt this lady in any way, I'll come back and bury you."

It was hard to say who was more surprised, Swill or Mabel. She grinned in delight and elevated her glass in a mock toast. "Let's hear it for the gentleman. Too bad there aren't more with his manners."

Swill tore off the second holdout and slammed it down. "Can I go now?"

"There just one more thing," Fargo said, and slugged the cardsharp across the jaw. He put all his weight into the punch, and it knocked both Swill and Swill's chair to the floor where the card slick lay in a crumpled pile, like so much dirty laundry. Then, grabbing Swill by the scruff of the shirt, Fargo dragged him to the oak door, opened it, and delivered a well-placed kick that rolled Swill out into the dust.

Denton ushered broken-nose and the last no-account outside. The pair radiated hatred like the setting sun radiated light. "How do we make sure these polecats don't sneak back and back-shoot us?"

Fargo's pinto stallion was at the hitch rail along with four others horses. "Which one is yours?" he asked.

"The sorrel," the gambler said.

Which meant the other three had to belong to Swill and his friends. Fargo went from one to the other, yanking rifles from saddle scabbards. His arms laden, he carried the weapons into the saloon, dropped them on a table, and came back out.

The man with the busted nose was gnashing his teeth in impotent frustration. "We'll get you for this, mister," he barked, the words distorted by the hands over his face. "No matter how long it takes, we'll make you eat crow."

"Maybe we should just blow windows in their skulls," Denton suggested, and elevated the pepperbox.

Fargo had half a mind to agree. But he wasn't a man-killer by nature. He only killed when others left him no other choice. Besides, he was heading west at first light. "Why waste the lead?" he responded. To Swill he said, "Light a shuck before I change my mind."

"And if you know what's good for you," the gambler added, "you won't show your faces here until long after we're gone."

The third local nudged the man with the broken nose. "Come on, Porter. Let's get the hell out of here while we still can."

"I'll go, Gib," Porter growled. "But I don't like running off with my tail tucked between my legs. I don't like it at all."

Fargo didn't holster his Colt until their mounts were lost in the distance. Two other men had come out of the stable and four more had wandered out of the general store to watch, but no one interfered. As Fargo turned to go inside one of the on-lookers bustled across, a stocky man with a droopy mustache and a white apron that pegged him as the store's owner.

"Pardon me, mister. I'm Sam Ziegler. I don't meant to pry, but I'm sort of the closest thing Les Bois has to a civic leader, and it's my duty to try and keep everyone in line." Ziegler poked a thumb northward. "What was that all about?"

"They were cheating at cards," Fargo said.

"Do tell." Ziegler didn't sound the least bit surprised. "I reckon they were bound to get caught sooner or later. The last wagon train that came through, Gus Swill took a pilgrim for pretty near two hundred dollars."

Fargo had little interest in the cheat's accomplishments. He went to go in, but Ziegler wasn't done.

"Has anyone told you about Swill's brothers? He's got eight of 'em and they're all as sidewinder-mean as he is. They live back up in the Seven Devils Mountains. Those fellers he was with, Ike Porter and Tim Gib, are pards of theirs. A dangerous bunch to have mad at you, I can tell you that."

"Thanks for the warning," Fargo said. Denton had already gone in, and he could hear Mabel's high-pitched laughter.

"Some of us don't cotton to the doings around here, is all," Ziegler said. "The Swills and their friends tend to ride roughshod over the rest of us and there's not a whole hell of a lot we can do about it."

"That's too bad." Fargo took another step but stopped at the next words out of the storekeep's mouth.

"You could do something, though. Any hombre who can run off Gus Swill has to have more sand than a desert. What would you say if we offered to hire you to take care of all the Swills?"

Fargo glanced over his shoulder. "Take care of them?"

"Get rid of them permanently," Ziegler elaborated. "Some towns hire regulators to dispose of their vermin. We'd like to do the same." With a wave of his hand, Ziegler included the onlookers. "How would you like the job?"

"This is awful sudden," Fargo commented. They didn't know him from Adam and must be desperate for help. But just as he wouldn't gun Swill and the others down in cold blood, he had never hired out as an assassin and he wasn't going to start now.

"If you only knew," Ziegler said. "We've been looking for the right man for over a year now. About eight weeks ago we thought we'd found him. A cowboy drifted in from down Texas way. He was a hardcase riding the owl-hoot trail, or so he claimed, and we thought he'd be perfect. We outfitted him with a new rifle and plenty of ammunition and all the grub he'd need, and off into the Devils he went." Ziegler frowned. "He never came back."

"Maybe he was playing you for fools," Fargo said. "Maybe he took that new rifle and kept going."

"We suspected as much," Ziegler said, "until his horse showed up, half-lame and half-starved. The saddle was coated with dry blood." He came closer and lowered his voice. "So what do you say? Between us we can afford to pay you seven hundred dollars. Not a bad grubstake."

Not bad at all, Fargo reflected, and proof they must *really* want the Swills dead. "I'm not your man," he said, and entered the saloon before Zielger could bend his ear some more. Denton was at the same table, playing solitaire. Mabel and Barnes were at the counter, nursing drinks. Fargo snatched up his glass and walked over for a refill.

"That was mighty nice of you to speak up on my behalf," Mabel thanked him. "I can't recollect the last time a man did that for me."

Fargo leaned on the plank and gave her a new scrutiny. Her breasts were larger than most and swelled against her dress as if trying to burst out. Full hips and nicely shaped thighs were outlined by the silken fabric. His groin twitched at the images he conjured of her lying naked in an inviting pose.

Mabel inched up to him and playfully placed a forefinger on his chest. Her eyes hooded, she cooed, "I'd like to thank you for what you did."

"That's not necessary," Fargo assured her.

"Maybe not." Mabel glanced below his belt and rimmed her full lips with the pink tip of her tongue. "But it sure would be a night you'd remember."

No other series has this much historical action!

THE TRAILSMAN

☐ #211: BADLANDS BLOODBATH   0-451-19694-5
☐ #212: SIOUX STAMPEDE   0-451-19757-7
☐ #214: TEXAS HELLION   0-451-19758-5
☐ #215: DUET FOR SIX-GUNS   0-451-19866-2
☐ #216: HIGH SIERRA HORROR   0-451-19860-3
☐ #217: DAKOTA DECEPTION   0-451-19759-3
☐ #218: PECOS BELLE BRIGADE   0-451-19891-3
☐ #219: ARIZONA SILVER STRIKE   0-451-19932-4
☐ #220: MONTANA GUN SHARPS   0-451-19964-2
☐ #221: CALIFORNIA CRUSADER   0-451-19977-4
☐ #223: IDAHO GHOST-TOWN   0-451-20024-1
☐ #224: TEXAS TINHORNS   0-451-20041-1
☐ #225: PRAIRIE FIRESTORM   0-451-20072-1
☐ #226: NEBRASKA SLAYING GROUND   0-451-20097-7
☐ #227: NAVAJO REVENGE   0-451-20133-7
☐ #228: WYOMING WAR CRY   0-451-20148-5
☐ #229: MANITOBA MARAUDERS   0-451-20164-7
☐ #230: FLATWATER FIREBRAND   0-451-20202-3
☐ #231: SALT LAKE SIREN   0-451-20222-8
☐ #234: APACHE DUEL   0-451-20281-3
☐ #235: FLATHEAD FURY   0-451-20298-8
☐ #237: DAKOTA DAMNATION   0-451-20372-0
☐ #238: CHEROKEE JUSTICE   0-451-20403-4
☐ #239: COMANCHE BATTLE CRY   0-451-20423-9
☐ #240: FRISCO FILLY   0-451-20442-5
☐ #241: TEXAS BLOOD MONEY   0-451-20466-2

To order call: 1-800-788-6262